MURDER

ON THE PENINSULA

Irish crime fiction you won't be able to put down

DAVID PEARSON

Paperback edition published by

The Book Folks

London, 2019

© David Pearson

ISBN 978-1-0726-1497-5

www.thebookfolks.com

For Joan.

Chapter One

It had been a good summer. The weather had been amazing, with what seemed like endless sunny days and temperatures into the high twenties. But as Senior Inspector Maureen Lyons looked out the window of the Garda station in Mill Street, it was clear that autumn now had a good grip on the city.

Thick grey clouds hung over the place, and if it wasn't actually raining, it wasn't far off. The stiff south-westerly breeze had an edge to it, causing pedestrians to grip their overcoats tightly around them. Still, the change in seasons brought its own reward. The tourist traffic had all but stopped, and the insanity that marked the start of Christmas hadn't yet begun. Sure, they would have Halloween to cope with shortly, but that was mostly exuberant youths being silly with fireworks smuggled down from Northern Ireland, and enormous bonfires set up on any available open space in between the tightly packed houses of the council estates. Uniform could deal with all of that.

From Lyons' perspective, it had been a fruitful time too. Her partner, Superintendent Mick Hays, had finally produced a detective sergeant to fill the long-standing vacancy. He was a young man from Cork who, to Lyons, looked to be barely out of school. Lyons had interviewed him with Inspector Eamon Flynn and they had to agree that what Galway folks said about Cork people appeared to be epitomized in the young man. He was smart – very smart – even if his sing-song accent and youthful appearance belied the fact.

Superintendent Hays had also had a good summer. With his duties now largely administrative, he had managed to get out in his beloved boat almost every weekend. The gentle on-shore breezes made sailing in and around Galway Bay a delightful experience, and he had even persuaded Maureen to come out with him a few times, although she didn't normally enjoy being at sea. Still, she had to admit, it could be idyllic as the little boat cut through the waves without any drama, and even when the breeze got up a bit, the Folkboat's clever design, with its steeply cutaway bow, ensured that both skipper and crew remained dry on board. And there was no better way to work up an appetite. Hays had been talking about upgrading the Folkboat, as the maintenance on the wooden hull was becoming arduous. But any such upgrade would be costly, and he couldn't justify the outlay for the moment.

* * *

Garda Mary Fallon, the latest addition to the force who had been allocated to Sergeant Séan Mulholland's station in Clifden, was driving to work in Roundstone along the coast road. After her posting to Clifden, Mulholland had decided that she would be of more benefit working out of Roundstone, where up to that time Garda Pascal Brosnan had been running the little Garda station at the edge of the village single-handedly. So, Mary commuted each morning from her accommodation on the edge of Clifden to Roundstone. It was only a twenty-minute drive into the village, and it was a nice enough journey on most days. There were two possible routes, but Mary always went around by Ballyconneely, as she liked to look out at the sea as she drove along. Being from County Kilkenny herself, she wasn't used to seeing the sea too often, and it gave her a lift to watch the constant motion, and the waves breaking on the shore with screaming seabirds overhead.

As she drove along that morning in her old but reliable Volkswagen Golf, she glanced to her right when passing the beach at Ballyconneely. She was surprised to see the usual uninterrupted view to the horizon punctuated with a dark shape that appeared to be stationery on the surface of the waves. This had not been there the previous day, so Mary pulled the car over to the side of the road and got out for a better look.

The tide was ebbing, and after a few more minutes she could see that the shape was the roof of a car, the side windows now coming occasionally into view as the waves retreated. Mary took out her mobile phone, but there was no signal. She hadn't yet switched to the service that provided reception all over the remote region. She would have liked to have phoned back to Clifden, or even to Pascal Brosnan for guidance as to what to do, but she had no luck. She got back into the car, turned around, and drove to where the Alcock and Brown memorial stood at

Derrygimlagh. She drove up past the memorial itself to higher ground where a large flat patch of loose gravel served as a makeshift car park for visitors and the occasional tour bus that came to see where the two intrepid airmen had found land. Mary was glad to see that there were now two bars of reception on her phone. She decided to call Pascal.

"Hi, Pascal. It's Mary here. I'm on my way in, but I stopped at Ballyconneely. There seems to be a car out on the beach, and the tide has come in over it. What should I do?"

"Ah, you're grand, Mary. We get one or two of those every year. Some eejit probably drove out there with his girlfriend last night and didn't notice the tide coming in around him, and then he'd be properly stuck in the sand. What way is the tide going?" Brosnan said.

"It's going out, I think. But what if there's someone in it?"

"Don't be daft girl. Sure, wouldn't they get out as soon as they knew what was happening? No, wait till you see, the fella will turn up looking sheepish in Clifden, or here, later on looking for help. What he doesn't realise is that the car is a goner. Even if it can be got out, the sea has it destroyed. Is it old or new?"

"I can't tell, Pascal. It's still mostly submerged. But are you sure there's nothing to be done?" Mary said.

"Nothing you can do anyway, Mary. I'll give the council a call later on and they'll get a tractor out to pull it free. They don't like leaving them there like that – it looks bad for the tourists."

"You don't think I should have a closer look then?"

"No, there's no need. And besides, unless you have your swimsuit with you, you'd get soaked. No. Come on into work and I'll deal with it."

"Yeah, OK. See ya."

Mary got back into her car and drove back down to the N341 and on the rest of the way into Roundstone, parking beside the small modern Garda station on the outskirts of the village. When she went inside, Pascal Brosnan had the teapot ready on the stove and they had a cup together.

"So, what have we on today, Pascal?" she said.

"Nothing much. One of us will have to go down to the hotel a bit later. There's been some pilfering going on at the back of the place, and they want us to put in an appearance. I'd say it's one of their own staff, but maybe seeing a uniform hanging around a bit will put a stop to it."

"Right. I can do that, if you like. But would you do something for me?"

"Go on," Brosnan said, sensing that he wouldn't like what was coming.

"I have an uneasy feeling about that car out beyond. Could we go out and have a look?"

"Mary, I don't want to piss on your chips, but there'll be nothing in it. I've seen a good few of these, and they're always just some daft bugger being stupid. Usually a visitor."

"I don't know, Pascal, I just got the shivers when I saw it. Humour me, would you? It'll only take a few minutes, and then I'll leave it, I promise."

"Jesus, girl, you don't give up, do you? OK, OK, have it your way. But if it turns out to be nothing, that's a pint you owe me – no, two pints. Deal?"

"Deal," Mary said, smiling.

Chapter Two

The two Gardaí put the customary notice on the door of the Roundstone Garda station, advising people to call Clifden if they needed urgent help; locked the front door, and set off in the white Hyundai squad car for Ballyconneely.

The early morning rain had moved east to Galway as they drove up past Dog's Bay where the beautiful white, horse-shoe shaped beaches glistened in the sunshine, with just a few cotton wool clouds skimming the tip of Errisbeg.

Brosnan was a bit frustrated at having to demonstrate to his new colleague that his experience could be relied upon to show that there was nothing to this sunken vehicle. But he enjoyed her company too, so it wasn't all bad. It was nice to get out of the confines of the station, and it was a pleasant drive in any case.

Fifteen minutes later, Brosnan pulled the car into the side of the road where there was a viewing point adjacent to Ballyconneely beach. The tide had gone out a good bit more since Fallon had been there earlier, and the vehicle that was stuck up to its waist in sand was now clearly visible some 300 metres offshore.

They got out of their car and set off across the strand. It was wet underfoot, with seawater lying on the sand between the ridges left by the departing tide. Here and there puddles had formed, and before they had gone very far, both Garda's shoes were soaking wet.

"I hope you're right about this, Mary. I'll never get the water marks out of these brogues!"

Fallon said nothing, walking on towards the semi-sunken shape.

As they got close, they could see that a depression had been created all around the forlorn car, and it was half-full of seawater. The vehicle itself, which appeared to be largely intact, apart from the fact that the roof had been bashed in by the waves, had sunk up to its waist-line in the sand. They walked around the car, noting that the windows appeared to be steamed up, so that it was difficult to see anything inside.

"I suppose I'd better wade in and see what's what," Mary said. She was hoping that Pascal Brosnan would be chivalrous enough to volunteer, but it didn't happen. Mary took off her shoes and socks, and rolled up her uniform trousers to the knee. She then gingerly stepped into the water surrounding the car, edging her way forward until she could lean on the roof and peer in. It was very hard to see anything inside, so she took her torch from her belt and shone it into the interior.

"I can't see anything much, Pascal. Should I break the window?" she said.

"Go for it. I don't think the insurance company will complain," Brosnan replied, chuckling to himself at the girl's persistence.

Mary took the torch in her right hand, and shielding her eyes with her left forearm, she smacked the side window of the car hard. The glass shattered, scattering tiny pieces all over the driver's seat, and a round hole the size of a football appeared in the window. Mary took the torch and shone it inside the vehicle.

"Jesus! Oh my God," she shrieked, and turning away from the car, holding her hand to her face, she bent forward and proceeded to vomit.

Alarmed by his colleague's behaviour, Brosnan waded in, shoes and all, to see what she had found. He took Mary's torch from her, and peered inside the sunken car. There, the cold glassy eyes of a dead girl were staring up at him. Her lower half was submerged in the seawater that had ingressed into the car, but her upper half was out of the water, slouched against the back of the passenger's seat. Brosnan could see that she was dead. Her skin had a plastic-like sheen to it, and was grey in pallor. Her lips were blue and slightly parted, revealing bright white teeth, and her clothing was opened, with her bra pushed up revealing her bare breasts. Her arms were floating in the seawater, giving her body movement which looked incongruous given that life had left her some time ago.

Brosnan stood back from the car.

"Good God, are you OK, Mary?"

"Yes, fine, sorry. I just got such a shock. I'll be fine," she said, although she looked very pale.

"Here, we'd better call this in. I think my phone should have a signal. Looks like I owe you a pint," he said, trying to cheer his colleague up a little.

Brosnan called Clifden and spoke to Sergeant Mulholland, explaining what they had found. Mulholland said he would get the fire brigade and the ambulance out at once, and then he'd notify Galway who would no doubt want to attend the scene.

"What way is the tide, Pascal?" Mulholland asked.

"I'd say it's turned, anyway. But it's a good bit out yet. I'd give it another hour and a half, and then we'll have to swim for it."

"Right. I'll tell them to get a move on so. Don't touch anything till they get there, but stay where you are. Is Mary OK?" Mulholland said.

"Ah, she'll be fine. It was her idea you know, to come out and investigate. She's had a shock, but she'll be OK in a few minutes."

"Hmph. I suppose they'd call that woman's intuition. Anyway, it's just as well one of you was a bit curious!" Mulholland said.

* * *

It was fifteen minutes later when the fire engine and ambulance pulled up on the verge at the access to the beach. Two paramedics in green jumpsuits came jogging across the sand towards the car, followed by two firemen in full regalia making more sedate progress due to the bulk of their cumbersome attire.

After a quick appraisal of the scene, the lead paramedic said to the two Gardaí, "There's not much we can do for this poor lassie, I'm afraid. Let's see if Jim can get her out."

Jim, the leading hand from the fire engine, arrived at the scene. He had a look around and then issued some instruction to his helper who set off back to the fire tender moving as quickly as his clobber would allow.

"We'll have to take the roof off to get her out. The doors are jammed closed by the sand. I'll start by pulling out the front and back windscreens, then when Paddy gets back with the pneumatic gear, we'll cut through the A posts and see if we can peel the roof back. I don't want to damage the poor girl any more than we have to."

Jim set to inserting a jemmy in between the windscreen rubber and the car's body, and leveraging the windscreen clear. It cracked in a crazed pattern as he pulled at it, and after a minute or two, it finally yielded and came away in his hand. He placed it on the driest part of the sand that he could find, and Mary Fallon took close-up photographs of the tax disc and insurance details from the broken windscreen using her mobile phone camera.

By the time Paddy had returned with the pneumatic metal cutters, Jim had the back window out too, and the pair set about cutting through the metal holding the roof in place. After a lot of grinding and groaning from the stricken car, a loud snap told the group that the required pieces had been severed. They hauled on the roof section, folding it back sufficiently to allow access to the passenger area of the car.

Mary Fallon was greatly impressed by the care taken by the firemen and the ambulance crew removing the body of the girl. They gently eased her out through the gap where the roof had once been, and laid her down on the open body bag that had been spread out on the sand to receive her. The female paramedic covered the girl's upper torso with a muslin cloth without disturbing her clothing, to give her a little more dignity.

"She was a nice-looking girl too. It's a shame," the woman said as she moved the girl's sodden hair away from her face.

Mary Fallon, now fully recovered from the shock of finding the dead body, was back at the side of the car. She reached in and collected a few pieces of paper that were floating in the muddy seawater inside, and took out a woman's shoe, putting it all into a large evidence bag. She then rolled up her sleeves and plunged her arm deep into the interior, opening the glove compartment of the car and removing the contents which went into the evidence bag along with the other stuff.

"Where are you taking the body?" Brosnan said.

"We'll take her in to the mortuary at the regional hospital in Galway. That way Dr Dodd doesn't have to travel all the way out here. And we'd better get a shift on, the tide is coming back in," the senior paramedic said.

"Right, so. We'll come on in too," Brosnan said.

* * *

Senior Inspector Maureen Lyons was in her office spending time planning and re-organising her expanded team. She would remain directly in charge of Detective Inspector Eamon Flynn. Flynn would be ably assisted by Detective Sergeant Sally Fahy, while the new man from Cork, Dermot Heffernan, would look after the two Detective Gardaí, Liam Walsh and Mary Costelloe, reporting to Flynn. In this way, Lyons could rely on two permanently active units, enabling them to deal more effectively with whatever presented itself. It also gave

Eamon Flynn a more significant role, which Lyons was sure he would relish, and it allowed her to step back slightly from front-line operations.

But for now, she was short-handed. Flynn had been sent off to Dublin on a training course, and Mary Costelloe was taking a fortnight's holiday; so Lyons had to get by temporarily with Sally Fahy, Liam Walsh, the young Dermot Heffernan, her newest recruit, along with John O'Connor – the team's technical expert. Lyons wasn't too bothered by the arrangements. With the tourist season over, and things fairly quiet in the area, they'd get by for a week or two till they were back up to strength. She was just putting the finishing touches to the roster that would accommodate all these variables, when Séan Mulholland telephoned her to bring her up to date with the developments out at Ballyconneely.

Mulholland was in his late fifties and could have retired from the force on full pension some years previously. But he was a single man and lived on his own, so he preferred to continue working where he felt useful. He enjoyed the camaraderie and the certain amount of status in the community that his position in the Gardaí afforded him.

When Lyons had been fully updated, she thanked the sergeant for letting him know, and said she would call Pascal Brosnan directly.

Brosnan answered the phone on the third ring.

"Hi Pascal, this is Inspector Lyons here. I understand you've found a body out in Ballyconneely."

"Yes, boss. We're just here now. The ambulance is taking her back into Galway. We had to cut the car open to get her out."

"Is there any evidence you can collect from the scene?" Lyons said.

"Mary has lifted some stuff from the car. We can't see the number plates, but we have the details from the discs in the windscreen. We're going to come in with the ambulance, is that OK?"

"Yes, that's fine. Take some photographs of the scene for me, will you? I'll ask Séan to get some men out to start asking around if anyone saw anything. How long do you think it's been there?"

"I'd say they stopped here during low tide last night. That would have been between about ten and twelve, give or take."

"Is there any sign of the driver?" Lyons said.

"No, not a trace."

"Is the vehicle recoverable?"

"No, boss. It's stuck in the sand up to its middle, and it's destroyed now after the firemen took the roof off. It'll probably disappear altogether with the next tide, which is just coming in now."

"OK. Well, can you report to me when you get here? And bring Mary with you."

"Right, boss. Will do."

Lyons knew that every year one or two cars got stuck in the sand out on the beautiful beaches west of Roundstone. It was usually tourists – the natives being well aware of the danger and carefully avoiding it. But in all the years that she had been working for the Gardaí in Galway, Lyons had never known there to be anything really sinister with these events – until now. Her curiosity with unexplained goings on was piqued, and she wondered if there was, once again, murderous activity in play out west.

Chapter Three

Brosnan pulled the squad car out in front of the ambulance and they drove off towards Galway. A small group of onlookers had gathered at the exit from the beach, but the Gardaí ignored them. They would be left to the two other men from Clifden to provide any information that they might have, but in all probability, they were just rubberneckers.

The sombre little convoy took almost an hour to reach the city. As they approached Galway, the rain set in again, adding to their already gloomy mood. They didn't use their lights or sirens – no amount of haste would do the dead girl any good now.

The ambulance unloaded its cargo at the mortuary behind the regional hospital, wheeling the gurney indoors to where Dr Julian Dodd was waiting.

"Ah, good day, Pascal. Inspector Lyons tells me you have been collecting corpses out in beautiful Ballyconneely," Julian Dodd said. He was dressed in a green rubber apron and standing by a stainless-steel bench

– his normal workplace. Dodd always seemed to have an unsuitable comment to make in these situations. But when you got past the smart remarks, he was a very fine pathologist. His evidence had nailed many a wayward killer over the years, and the detectives were glad to have him, despite his often acerbic demeanour. Dodd enrolled the assistance of two more junior pathologists to transfer the body bag to the mortician's table, and they unzipped and cut away the plastic, leaving the body of the girl lying on the cold metal slab.

"Thanks for bringing her in," Dodd said, "I must get on. Tell your boss I'll have preliminaries before tea time." He turned his attention to his latest specimen.

* * *

The two Gardaí drove the short distance to Mill Street station and went in search of Senior Inspector Lyons.

"Hi. Come on in. Take a seat," Lyons said when they appeared at her door. "So, what's the story?"

Pascal Brosnan told Lyons how Mary had insisted on going back out to where she had seen the sunken car on her way into work, and how they had discovered the body of the Jane Doe half-submerged in the sunken wreck. Lyons questioned Pascal and Mary about everything they had observed, and any evidence that they had discovered.

"When the firemen had removed the windscreen, I took these pictures of the discs in the window, and I retrieved some of the paperwork. They have the registration number and insurance details of the car," Fallon said, extending her iPhone across the table for Lyons to see, and placing the evidence bag with the damp papers in it on the desk.

"Well done, Mary. That was quick thinking. You must have got an awful fright."

"It's the first time I've seen a corpse in the line of duty, Inspector. Yes, it was horrible, but I suppose you get used to it eventually," Fallon said.

"Not really, Mary, we never get totally used to this kind of thing. I guess it's just as well, otherwise we would become complacent, and there's no room for that in our line of work."

Lyons turned to John O'Connor who was standing patiently by.

"John, take these and see who owns this car, will you? And see if you can find out anything more from these bits and pieces," Lyons said.

"Right, boss. Is it OK to dry them out on the heater?"

"Yes, of course, but make sure they are preserved. They may be important."

"Right, boss. I'll let you know."

"OK, Pascal. If there's nothing else, you should get back out to Roundstone. But keep your ear to the ground. See what the gossip in the village is about the incident. And see if there's any talk about who the girl might be – we need to identify her as soon as possible. We'll take it from here. And thanks, Mary. That was a good piece of detective work – well done to you both."

* * *

Just as Sergeant Séan Mulholland was about to break for lunch, a couple in their fifties came into the station. Mulholland recognised them, although he wasn't by any stretch a friend of theirs. The couple ran one of several gift shops in the town, and he had met them in the shop and seen them around the place from time to time.

"Ah, hello. Mr and Mrs Finnegan, isn't it? And what can I do for you folks today?" Mulholland said cheerily.

"Hello, Sergeant. I hope we're not wasting your time but, you see, it's Sheena," Mr Finnegan said.

"Sheena. Yes, eh, remind me who exactly Sheena is?"

"Our daughter, of course. She's lived with us ever since she finished university last year," Mrs Finnegan said. It was clear that the pair expected Mulholland to know all about their small family.

"Oh, right. And what is it about Sheena then?" Mulholland said.

"Well, that's just it, she didn't come home last night, and she hasn't been in touch since, and she's not at work. We're very worried. It's not like her at all," Mr Finnegan said.

"I see. And where was Sheena last night?"

"She went out at about nine to meet some of her friends in the town. One of them had a birthday – Carol, I think it was – and they went out for a meal, and I suppose a few drinks. We assumed she had come home, but when we checked her room this morning, she wasn't there, and she's not at work either. We don't usually hear her coming in if she's out late. We're heavy sleepers," Mrs Finnegan said.

"And have you contacted this Carol yourselves?"

"No. She works in Letterfrack, at the hotel, and we wouldn't like to call her at work in case she might get into trouble," Mr Finnegan said.

"Where does Sheena work?"

"She works in the council offices here in the town. She got the job after she'd finished her degree. She's in administration," Mrs Finnegan said proudly.

"And I presume you called the council office?" Mulholland said. He was finding it hard to detect any urgency in the parents' actions, which struck him as a bit odd.

"Oh, yes, we did. But she hasn't been in. They thought she might be a bit hungover after the night out, and was taking the morning off," Mrs Finnegan said.

"Right. Well what's this Carol's surname then?" Mulholland asked. He was becoming concerned and frustrated at the same time with these two gentle people.

Mrs Finnegan turned plaintively to her husband.

"Don't look at me. I hardly know the girl," the man said.

Mulholland intervened before the woman had a chance to respond.

"Don't worry. I'll call the hotel and talk to her. Now, if I could just have your contact details, I'll get working on this at once. We'll treat it as a missing person case till we find out what's happened to Sheena. But I'm sure there's a perfectly reasonable explanation, so try not to worry."

The Finnegans exchanged concerned looks, and Mr Finnegan took the sheet of paper that Mulholland had placed in front of him on the counter and wrote down their address and mobile phone numbers in a rather shaky hand.

"Thanks, Mr Finnegan. I'll be in touch as soon as I have any information," Mulholland said.

As soon as the Finnegans had left the Garda station, Mulholland called Lyons back in Galway and explained the recent encounter.

"OK, Séan. I'd better get out there pronto. It sounds like that could be the girl in the car all right. I'll get Pascal to send me one of the photos he took at the scene. I'll send it on to you and see if you can get the identification confirmed locally. I'll see you there shortly. Oh, and while I'm driving out, will you contact this Carol and see what she has to say for herself? Get as much detail as you can, especially around the end of the night – how they all got home and so on," Lyons said.

Lyons collected Sally Fahy from the open plan office and told her they were going to Clifden in connection with the dead girl.

Before she left, John O'Connor came across to speak to her.

"Inspector, I have the details of that car you asked about," O'Connor said.

"Great. What's the story?"

"It belongs to a hire company – Celtic Car Hire. It was rented by a man called John Hughes at their Galway office a few days ago. They are sending me his address and other details now. He took it for a week. He said his own car was in for repair. But there is something odd," O'Connor said.

"What's that?"

"He apparently paid in cash. He had some story about his credit card being lost, so he paid a €500 deposit and €150 for the rental, all in cash."

"Didn't that ring alarm bells with the agent?" Lyons said.

"Yes, but they said that there wasn't much happening at the moment given the time of year, and the chance to get a car out for a week was too much to turn down."

"Great! Have we a photo of Mr Hughes?"

"No, but they're sending a scan of his driving license across to me as well. I'll have it in about an hour."

"OK. When you get the address, ask Liam to check it out. He can take a uniformed Garda with him if it's anywhere nearby."

* * *

"Just my luck for this to happen when we're short-handed, Sally," Lyons said as they drove out on the all-too-familiar N59 towards Clifden in Lyons' Volvo.

"I know what you mean, but we can always get help if it turns awkward. Anyway, it might just be an unfortunate accident."

"Maybe. We'll see," Lyons said, unconvinced.

The phone rang in the car which Lyons was able to answer by pressing a button on the steering wheel.

"It's Julian Dodd here, Inspector. I thought you might like to know the cause of death for the girl that was brought in earlier."

"Hi, Doc; yes please."

"Well, the odd thing is she didn't drown. Not a drop of the great Atlantic Ocean in her lungs. But there is some bruising beginning to appear around the neck. If I was given to guessing, which as you know I am not, I'd say it's possible that she may have been strangled. I'll know more tomorrow when I have completed some more tests."

"I see. Any idea of the time of death?" Lyons said.

"Difficult to be precise with all that water around. It distorts the natural cooling process and the development of bacteria in the cadaver; I'd say between nine and midnight yesterday, but that's only an informed approximation," Dodd said.

"Hmmm, well that ties in with the tides, I guess. Anything else of note?" Lyons said.

"By that I take it you mean recent sexual activity, that sort of thing."

"Well?"

"No. Nothing obvious anyway. It's just possible a condom was used and the seawater washed away any residue, but unlikely, in my view, and the girl's underwear was still where it ought to be. There is one odd thing though. One of her front teeth was broken. We found it lodged in her throat."

"Was it broken off through violence?" Lyons said.

"I've no idea, inspector. That's for you to find out. I'm just a humble medical man."

"Thanks, Doctor. What about her stomach?"

"Looks like spaghetti carbonara. Partly digested, so probably about two to three hours before death. Oh, and a good quantity of white wine. Hardly vintage, but lots of it."

"Would she have been intoxicated then?" Lyons said.

"I can't say. People absorb alcohol at very different rates, and what with the food and everything, but I'd say she was certainly feeling the effects."

"OK. Thanks, Doc. If anything else comes up, please let me know, won't you?"

"Of course, Inspector; as always."

Chapter Four

Lyons and Fahy made their way into the Garda station in Clifden where Sergeant Séan Mulholland was just settling down to a cup of tea.

"Hello, folks. Would you like a cuppa?" Mulholland said.

"No, we're grand, Séan. Did you get the photograph I sent you of the dead girl?"

"Yes, I did, Maureen, and it's Sheena Finnegan all right. I got the parish priest to verify it – he'll be very discreet, don't worry," Mulholland said.

"Right, you and me need to get out to the Finnegans' and break the bad news. Sally – will you stay here and see what Peadar and Jim have turned up from their enquiries?" Lyons said, all business like.

"Ah, would you not take one of the lads out with ye, Maureen? I'm no good at this kind of thing, and it will be good practice for them," Mulholland said.

"Afraid not, Séan. This is one for you and me. You know these people, and it would look very peculiar if two total strangers turned up out of the blue with this kind of message. Get your jacket and come on before they hear it from someone else. Do they live far outside the town?"

"No, not far. Just a wee bit up the Westport road and then a turn in to the left. It's called McCushla's Lane."

As Lyons and Mulholland pulled away in Lyons' car and drove down through the town towards the junction of the Westport road, Lyons noticed that a Nissan Qashqai had tucked in behind them. There were two male occupants, and the passenger had a camera resting on the dashboard with a very large pale grey coloured lens stuck on the front of it. Lyons dialled Fahy on her hands-free phone.

"Sally, I think I'm being followed by a couple of journos. We're just heading up onto the Westport road. Could you intercept them and slow them down a bit? It's a grey Nissan Qashqai, reg. number 151-D-96477."

"Sure, boss, looking forward to it already!"

"That's my girl. Thanks."

"We'll drive on up past this McCushla lane so as not to give our friends a clue. When Sally has dealt with them, we can double back. OK?" she said to Mulholland.

"Grand. Just carry on out the road for now," he said.

* * *

A couple of minutes later as they drove along the Westport road they heard sirens cutting through the still autumn air. The Qashqai made no effort to pull in, so Fahy, who was accompanied by Peadar Tobin, overtook it and cut in across its bows, causing the driver to stamp on the brakes to avoid hitting the Garda vehicle. Fahy and

Tobin jumped out of the car, with Fahy going to the driver's window and Tobin to the passenger's side.

Fahy showed her warrant card and demanded the driver's license, and any other paperwork he had for the vehicle. Tobin inspected the NCT disc and the insurance and tax discs displayed in the windscreen.

"Sergeant. The NCT is out of date. It ran out two months ago," Tobin called out.

Fahy had her notebook out, and was taking down the driver's details. The driver wasn't happy, and tried to get out of the vehicle, but Fahy told him to stay put, reaching in and removing the keys from the ignition.

She then went around to the boot and opened the tailgate. She noticed that there was no spare tyre in the well in the floor. Further inspection revealed that the two rear tyres were below the legal limit for tread depth.

When Fahy went back to the driver, who was becoming quite agitated, she said, "I'm sorry, sir, but I can't let you proceed any further in this vehicle. It's defective, and shouldn't be on the road. If you want to wait here with it, I'll arrange a tow for you back to a garage. They can supply a spare wheel and fit two new tyres. And you'll need to get the NCT done immediately too – that's a fixed penalty fine and three points on your license for starters."

The passenger was aiming his camera at Fahy and taking photographs of the proceedings. When she had finished remonstrating with the driver, she walked coolly round to the other side of the vehicle and demanded that the camera be handed over.

"I'm seizing the memory card out of this thing under section seven of the Criminal Justice Act. I believe it may be material to an ongoing investigation we are handling.

You can get it back by applying to Clifden Garda station when we are finished with it."

"You can't do that! This is police harassment. We're accredited journalists, you know!" the man in the passenger's seat protested.

Fahy remained silent until the man had finished his rant.

"If you want harassment, then that's no bother. I'm an expert in it. Would you like a strip search here on the side of the road, is that what you're after? But I warn you, any more of that shite out of you and I'll arrest you both for obstructing the Gardaí in the execution of their duty, and believe me, a bald tyre or two will be the least of your worries. Have you been in the cells in Clifden overnight? Quare things go on there, that's all I'm saying."

The two occupants of the Qashqai quietened down when they heard this. Fahy turned away till she was out of earshot and called Tadgh Deasy on her mobile phone. Deasy ran a garage of sorts out the far side of Roundstone, and had a tow truck that the Gardaí had called upon in the past. While Deasy's enterprise was not always squeaky clean, it suited the Gardaí well enough to let him go about his business for the odd occasion such as this where he could be helpful to them.

She told Deasy where they were and, making sure that the two were out of earshot, said, "and you can charge them a good few quid for the tow, the tyres and the spare wheel too. Rub it in as much as you like. They're a pair of right arrogant feckers."

"Thanks very much, Sergeant, we'll be out right away," Deasy said.

On the way back to the Clifden Garda station, Tobin said, "Remind me never to get on the wrong side of you, Sergeant!"

"Ah, you're grand, Peadar. My bark is worse than my bite, and those two were asking for it! Can you have a look at whatever is on the memory card from the camera just in case they may have captured something useful?"

* * *

When Lyons and Mulholland were happy that Fahy had taken care of the two journalists, they turned the car around and went back in towards Clifden.

"Here we are. Make a right turn here, Maureen," Mulholland said, gesturing with his right hand to a narrow unmetalled track.

Lyons turned the Volvo onto the path with grass and weeds growing up in the centre.

"It's the second house here on the left," Mulholland said, this time gesturing with his left hand.

Lyons strongly disliked these house calls bearing bad news to parents or relatives about their loved ones. Over twenty years previously, when Lyons was a fifteen-year-old schoolgirl, she had a very good friend by the name of Máiréad Nulty. She often went over to Máiréad's house after school to listen to music. Máiréad had been given a boom box for her birthday. It was a huge Sanyo thing in grey plastic, with detachable speakers at each end and two tape decks, so that you could listen to a music cassette and record it onto a blank tape at the same time. Lyons had made several bootleg copies of Máiréad's music using this technique. They had been listening to their favourite David Bowie album, when there was a heavy knock at the front door. Máiréad's mother was baking, and her hands and apron were covered in flour, so she asked Máiréad to see who it was. Their visitor was Sergeant Healy – a tall, well-built man, who had a full head of silver-grey hair when he took off his Garda cap.

"Can I come in, Máiréad. Is your mother at home?" he said, stepping into the hall.

Máiréad had a brother, Michael. He was three years older than she, and was what would have been described as a 'petrol head'. He was mad about anything mechanical, and his pride and joy was a Kawasaki 550GT motorcycle. When he wasn't riding it, he spent all of his time polishing the bright blue frame and shining the copious amounts of chrome on the mudguards and exhaust pipes. Lyons quite fancied Michael, but he had no time for girls – especially younger ones – he was dedicated to the bike and that was as far as his affections seemed to extend.

Mrs Nulty came out into the hall when she heard the deep voice of a man. When she saw who it was, she immediately became concerned.

"Ah, hello Sergeant. Won't you come in? I have the kettle on for a cup of tea, and there are scones just out of the oven."

"Ah, no thanks, Mrs Nulty. I won't if you don't mind. Is there somewhere we could have a word?" Healy said.

The upshot of the house call was that Máiréad's brother had been killed on his motorbike. He had hit a tree when he was unable to navigate a bad bend on a back-road into Athenry. The sergeant made a point of telling Mrs Nulty that there was a long skid mark on the road leading to the smashed-up bike, and although it wasn't specifically referred to, that was a coded message indicating that it had not been suicide.

Lyons remembered how the death of their eldest had destroyed the Nulty family almost completely. Máiréad became sullen and introverted, and her parents never recovered from the blight that the loss of their son had brought upon them. And now she was about to do the same for this family.

* * *

Lyons turned in through the narrow, rusty, wrought iron gates onto the gravel driveway of Finnegan's bungalow. The house was a small, double-fronted place covered in slightly tired pebble-dash. There was a rectangle of grass in front of it that looked as if it could do with one more cut before the growth stopped for the winter. The front door was set back in a small recess with a red brick arch in front of it, and dark red quarry tiles on the little porch that the arrangement provided. Lyons noticed that the windows were still the original ones that would have been supplied when the house was new back in the 1950s, giving the entire property a slightly uncared for look. A single chimney stack rose from the back of the house issuing blue turf smoke into the afternoon sky.

As they walked up to the front door, Lyons whispered to Mulholland, "You lead on this one, Séan." Mulholland didn't reply, but nodded to confirm that he understood.

The front door of the Finnegans' house was dark green, and the paint was no longer glossy, having faded in the sunshine and cracked here and there. The brass combination of letter box and door knocker were tarnished and pitted, but still functioned, so Mulholland rapped twice on the fixture.

It was Mrs Finnegan who answered. She was a small woman, with wiry grey hair, cut short. Her face was wrinkled, and her hands showed signs of age, with dark brown liver spots clearly visible. She wore a print dress that didn't really fit her anywhere; dark brown thick nylon stockings protruded from its hem, leading down to well-worn flat shoes.

"Hello, Sergeant, 'tis yourself. Won't you come in? The kettle is just boiled."

Mulholland introduced Lyons and the two followed Mrs Finnegan into the kitchen which was at the back of the house. Lyons noticed that the air in the house was none too fresh, a slight smell of boiled cabbage pervading the atmosphere. Mr Finnegan was seated on one of the four bare wooden rail-backed chairs reading the daily paper that was spread out on the oilcloth covering the table.

Greetings were exchanged, although Mr Finnegan didn't get up. Lyons noticed a photograph of a young girl propped up on the dresser that was home to the crockery and other clutter that collects in houses. The girl was in her college gown and mortarboard, smiling warmly for the camera.

"So, what about you?" said Mr Finnegan as the two Gardaí took their seats.

"Mr Finnegan, I'm sorry to say that the body of a young woman has been found out near Ballyconneely. Now, we have no confirmation at present, but there is a possibility that it could be Sheena," Mulholland said.

Mrs Finnegan dropped the earthenware teapot she had been warming on the hard, tiled floor, and it broke into several pieces.

"Oh, dear God, no," she wailed and sat down unsteadily on the only vacant chair, wringing her hands and clutching a rather grimy tea towel to her face. No one spoke for a minute or two, and then Lyons got up and completed the tea-making duties, putting tea bags directly into the mugs that Mrs Finnegan had left out.

"How sure are you, Sergeant?" Mr Finnegan said, closing his paper and looking directly at Séan Mulholland.

"Is this Sheena here?" Lyons interjected, pointing to the framed photograph she had spotted earlier.

"Yes, that's her. That was taken at her graduation in Galway last year," Finnegan said. "She has a degree, you know?"

"We can't be certain without formal identification, but the girl that was found does look very like the photograph. I'm sorry," Lyons said.

Mrs Finnegan had been rendered speechless by the sad news, but her husband managed to continue the conversation.

"What happened to her?" he said.

"We're not sure yet, Mr Finnegan. The body was discovered in a partly submerged vehicle out on the strand at Ballyconneely by one of my officers this morning. We'll need you to come into Galway to give us a formal identification, but tomorrow will do fine," Mulholland said.

"Dear God. What was she doing all the way over there? She only went out for a few drinks with her friends in the town. She would have been walking home after. I don't understand."

"Well, it's early days yet, Mr Finnegan. Our investigation is just getting started. We'll know more in a day or two," Mulholland said.

"Did she drown? Why didn't she get out of the car?" the man continued.

"We haven't established the circumstances of her death yet, Mr Finnegan, but there is a suggestion that foul play may have been involved. The pathologist will be able to advise us tomorrow."

"Foul play? What, do you mean she was killed by someone?" Finnegan said.

"It looks as if that may be the case, but we really can't say any more for now. Is there someone we can get to come over and be with you?" Lyons said, not wanting to go into any further details until more was known.

"Could you ask Father Meehan to come up to us?" Mrs Finnegan managed to say.

"Yes. Yes, of course. I'll call him right away. I'll stop by tomorrow at about ten o'clock and take you both into the hospital. I'm so sorry," Mulholland said, getting up from the table. He put his hand on the man's shoulder before going to the front door to call the priest.

Lyons carefully reversed the car back down onto McCushla Lane and turned it back towards Clifden.

"I think it's definitely her, OK. Don't you?" Lyons said.

"'Tis to be sure. God, it's an awful shame. She was a grand lass. Popular too. She had a good few friends in the town," Mulholland said.

"On the subject of which, did you manage to speak to that Carol girl?"

"No, I didn't. I called the hotel but they couldn't find her. They said she was there all right, but she could have been in one of the rooms cleaning or something. I left a message for her to call me when she reappeared."

"Why don't we go out there now, see if we can catch her? She may have some information," Lyons said.

Chapter Five

Carol Gleeson was just finishing her shift at the hotel in Letterfrack when Mulholland and Lyons arrived. They asked for her at reception, and a few minutes later a thin, fair-haired girl emerged from the staff area, wrapped in a lightweight raincoat. The three of them went into the lounge, which, at that time of day, was deserted. An open fire had been lit to make the room more welcoming, and the view from the picture windows out across the little harbour into the bay was magnificent, with the sun low in the autumn sky behind Inisbofin.

Mulholland broke the news of Sheena's death to Carol, who had been busy at the hotel all day, and hadn't heard anything about it.

"No, no, she can't be. I was with her just last night. Sheena can't be dead. It's not possible," she said, and started crying uncontrollably. Carol had gone very pale, so Lyons went off to get her a stiff brandy for fear that she would pass out, while Mulholland remained with her in an embarrassed silence.

When Lyons returned, Carol sipped the rich brown spirit, and some colour began to come back to her ghostly complexion.

"Can you tell us about last night, Carol? What time did you finish up in Clifden?" Lyons asked.

"I'm not totally sure," the girl said nervously. "I was on foot, because we had been drinking, but I'd say it was around midnight. I had an early shift here, so I didn't want to be too late."

"And did you leave the pub together – you and Sheena, I mean?"

"Yes. We left at the same time, but Sheena went off down the town towards the Westport Road – she lives out that way, and I went the other direction down Market Street to Bridewell Lane. That's where I'm from."

"So, the last time you saw Sheena was outside the pub at about twelve, yes?" Lyons asked.

"Yes, I guess so. But what happened to her?" Carol said, taking another sip of brandy as she recalled the moment.

"I'm really sorry Carol, but Sheena's body was recovered from a car out at Ballyconneely strand earlier today. We can't say anything more for the moment, but she didn't die of natural causes," Lyons said.

"Oh my God! The poor girl. Oh God, what about her poor mother and father? And her brother." Carol started to sob uncontrollably again.

When she had composed herself a little, and taken another good swig of the liquor, Mulholland asked, "Did you see any cars on the street, or anyone driving along beside Sheena?"

"Well, there were cars parked all over, but I never saw anyone driving along. The place was deserted except for ourselves." She blew her nose loudly into her white cotton handkerchief.

"Did Sheena have a boyfriend, Carol? Or was there anyone at work she was close to that you're aware of?" Mulholland said.

"No. No one special anyway. She had a few friends that are boys, but she wasn't dating or anything."

"OK. We'll need to get a list of those people from you."

"Yes, of course. But do you think we are safe in the town? You said you think she may have been killed – that's terrible. Is there a killer on the loose?"

"It's far too early to say, Carol. I'd say be a bit cautious after dark – try not to go about on your own for the next wee while, till we find out what's been going on. And don't under any circumstances get into any stranger's car. But there's no need to panic. This is a very unusual occurrence in these parts. Just be careful," Mulholland said.

Carol gave them a few names of men that she thought Sheena was known to from the town, and Mulholland wrote them down in his pocket book. They finished the interview, asking Carol if she was OK to drive home, and she assured them that she was. They left the hotel together, and Lyons drove Séan Mulholland back to the Garda station on the edge of Clifden.

"Get Jim Dolan to check out the names that she gave us. I don't think there'll be anything there, but best to check in any case. I need to get back into Galway. If the lads found anything, be sure to let me know, won't you?"

"Oh, of course I will, Maureen. Mind how you go now. See ya," Mulholland said, getting out of the car.

Fahy re-joined Lyons as the two set off for Galway.

"Thanks for looking after the two journos," Lyons said.

"I enjoyed that – pricks. Tadgh Deasy is dealing with them now, so they'll be a good bit poorer by the time the day is out!"

* * *

Back in the open plan office at Mill Street, Lyons spoke to her team. Superintendent Mick Hays slipped in at the back of the room and stood against the wall. He had obviously heard about the dead girl, and wanted to see what progress was being made.

"Right, let's not hang about. John, what have you got from the car hire?"

"Very little, boss. They sent across a scan of his license, but it's very poor. It could be anyone – just a black blob on the page really. The license is an Irish one, but the serial number isn't in the database, so it's probably a fake."

"And did they really let the car out without a credit card?" Lyons said.

"Yes. They said business was very slack, and it was better to get it out. It was a rental for a whole week, after all," O'Connor said.

"Well that was an expensive transaction. What was the car worth?" Fahy asked.

"It was new this year, so probably around €18,000 or so," O'Connor said.

A murmur of surprise went around the room.

"No gold star for that agent then. Anything else?" Lyons said.

"No, that's it. But Sergeant Heffernan has something."

"Great. Dermot?"

"Well, not much, to be honest. I went around to the address Hughes had given to the rental company. Nothing. It doesn't exist. There is a Cloonbeg Avenue, but it finishes at number 36, and he put 54 down as his address. We asked around, but no one had ever heard of John Hughes, and they said the house numbering hadn't been changed since the place was built in the 1970s."

"Is there a Cloonbeg Road or Park there as well?" Lyons said.

"No, just Avenue, and it's a cul-de-sac," Heffernan said.

"You mean a dead end," Fahy said straight-faced. There was a groan from the rest of the group.

"Did the lads out beyond get anything from their enquiries in Clifden?" Lyons said.

"No, boss, nothing. It seems it was just a normal night in the town. The pubs were doing OK, but not jammed or anything. They spoke to the barman where Sheena and Carol were drinking with their mates, but he said he didn't notice any strangers in the place, or anyone watching the girls. And they checked the hotels for a John Hughes to see if he was staying locally, but again nothing."

"OK. Thanks. Well, it seems we have a right old mystery on our hands. To summarize, some guy who we know almost nothing about has evidently killed a random stranger for no apparent reason, and he could be almost anywhere in the country by now. Or maybe he's lurking out west using a different alias, waiting to pounce again. This is not good, folks – not good at all. So, ideas?" Lyons said.

The detectives looked to one another for some spark of an idea, but none was forthcoming. After a few moments, Lyons spoke up again, "OK. So, no one has a clue – me neither, by the way. But we need some strategy to move this forward. Come on, give me something, guys."

After a few more minutes of embarrassed silence, Hays decided it was time to intervene. He caught Lyons' eye from the back of the room, and she gave him an almost imperceptible nod. Hays made his way to the front of the room, easing his passage between the chairs that were scattered around. He turned to face the small group.

"OK. I agree it's a puzzle, and from what I have heard, you have all done as much as you could so far. But it also occurred to me that this killing may not have been random at all. It seems to me that Hughes, or whatever his name is, went to a great deal of trouble to set this up. Either he intended to pick up someone off the street to murder, or the girl was specifically targeted. And depending on what happens over the next few days, we'll get the answer to that."

"What? Do you mean if there's another murder, then we'll know it was a random thing, but if there isn't, then Sheena was singled out?" Sally Fahy asked.

"Yes, something like that. We've known cases before where several people were murdered in quick succession to disguise the actual target – to make it look random, when it was anything but."

"So, are you saying that if there are more murders along the same lines, then possibly one of the victims is the real target, and the others are just to draw us off the scent?" Heffernan said.

"Exactly. Obviously, then, we continue our investigations as best we can with the little we've got, and wait to see what happens next. Back to you, Maureen," Hays said.

"Thanks, sir. Right, well, first thing tomorrow we'll put out an appeal for information. Pound the streets out in the area. Someone must have seen something. We'll get it on RTE as well. If we can't get anything from that, we may have to look at a reconstruction. I presume there's no CCTV anywhere out there?"

"No, boss," Fahy said.

"Right, we'll leave it at that for tonight. Let's crack on first thing tomorrow," Lyons said.

As the room cleared, Hays and Lyons walked back to her office. Hays closed the door.

"What do you think, Maureen?"

"God, I don't know, Mick. It seems all wrong to me. I mean, if he wanted just to kill a random stranger, why take her out to the beach in the car? Why not just drive up any one of the boreens nearby and do it there? And how did he lure the girl into the car in the first place? Surely she wasn't daft enough to take a lift from a total stranger late at night? She wasn't a silly teenager after all."

"Hmm. I see what you mean. So maybe they knew each other. But then all of the effort he went to hide his identity doesn't make sense," Lyons said.

"OK. Look, let's get out of here. We've had enough of this place for today. Let's go and get a nice meal and a drink, and I'll tell you all about my Folkboat woes to take your mind off it. This will still all be here in the morning. Get your coat."

"Yes, sir!"

Chapter Six

It had taken Eoin over an hour to get back to the old mobile home that he was using for shelter after he left the girl in the car. He had miscalculated the situation with the tides, and hadn't intended it to get stuck in the sand – but no matter. It would still serve his purpose.

He had found the deserted mobile home after a good deal of scouring the area when he arrived in Connemara a couple of weeks previously. It was perfect. Hidden from sight of any roads, and clearly no longer used, it had probably been abandoned a couple of years earlier. Still, there was some gas left in the yellow cylinder bottle that was rusting away slowly under the structure, and it had obviously been connected up to some type of well and drainage system, for there was a slow trickle of sweet water from the tap in the beige plastic sink in the kitchen area, and the toilet still flushed.

Eoin didn't dare to illuminate the interior of the caravan at night. Instead he used a single tea light on the worktop in the kitchen to punctuate the gloom. It was sufficient for him to see, but there wasn't enough output from the tiny candle to attract anyone's attention from outside.

His plan, so far, had worked out well. Picking up the girl had been all too easy. She was very drunk, tottering down through the town. He waited till she got clear of any possible cameras that there might be, and pulled the car in beside her.

"Which way are you going?" he had said, winding down the window on the passenger's side.

"Out the Westport road," she had responded, slurring her words.

"Me too. Hop in and I'll give you a lift," he said, and he opened the passenger's door invitingly.

The girl had more or less fallen into the car, and couldn't manage to fasten her seat belt, which was left loose by her side. As soon as the warmth of the interior hit her, she fell asleep, slouched back in the seat with her head lolling against the door.

Eoin had driven out along the back road to Ballyconneely, and parked on the beach. He had had a bit of fun with the girl who was totally oblivious, but when she woke up and started complaining, they struggled for a minute or two before the red mist descended and he punched her in the face and then strangled her with his bare hands. She hadn't put up much of a fight – she was out cold long before her last breath was taken.

"Perfect!" Eoin said to himself, as he started the car and tried to move off. But the tide had come in around the wheels, and no matter what he did, all that happened was that the vehicle dug in deeper and deeper into the sodden sand. Eventually, he got out and found himself calf deep in seawater. He left the scene and hurried back to the road, and then across the rocky fields to the old mobile home. He encountered no one on the way, though it took longer than he thought to make it home, and a fine drizzle had come down in the mist – helped along by a stiff south-westerly breeze – so that by the time he reached shelter he was soaked through.

As he pulled his damp clothes off and dried his hair in the grubby towel he had found in the bathroom, he said to himself, "Excellent. The trap is set!"

Chapter Seven

Lyons' first stop the following morning was at the mortuary where Dr Julian Dodd plied his gruesome trade.

"Morning, Doctor. I just called in to see if you found out anything more about Sheena Finnegan?"

"Hmm, let me see. Oh yes – the girl from the beach. Let's have a look." Dodd went across and pulled out one of the long stainless-steel drawers where his collection of dead bodies was stored. He pulled back the plain white cloth that was covering the girl to reveal her head and upper torso.

"As I suggested yesterday, the bruising around her throat is coming along nicely," he said, peering closely at the girl's bluish skin. "There are clear signs of vascular disruption on both sides of the neck. And there's an obvious hypostasis too, although I put that in my report yesterday," Dodd said.

"And what does all that mean in English, Doctor?"

"It means, dear lady, that the girl was almost certainly strangled by a human hand when she was reclining in the passenger's seat of the car with her feet on the floor. I would say that it was the perpetrator's right hand, judging by the impressions left by his or her thumb and forefinger. That's as much as I can tell you, I'm afraid."

"Could it have been a woman?" Lyons said.

"Well, unlikely. But we have to be politically correct these days, Inspector, so possibly, but I wouldn't bet your tea money on it," he said, looking at her over the tops of his glasses with a slight smirk.

"Would she have thrashed about as he strangled her?"

"It depends. She was pretty full of alcohol. She might have been completely out of it. But I can't see how that helps much."

"No, you're right. Me neither."

"There is one thing that might be of significance," Dodd said.

"Go on."

"One of her earrings is missing. Looks as if it was removed rather roughly post-mortem. It's one of those stud-like affairs with a small glass jewel in it. We have the other one if you'd like to have it."

"Yes please, Doc. Which one is it?"

"We have the one from the left ear. The missing one is, therefore, from her right ear which would have been the nearest to the perpetrator as they sat in the car."

"And how do you know it was removed after death?"

"No bleeding. Just the earlobe is torn, but it didn't bleed so her blood pressure was at zero by that time. The pump had stopped," Dodd said.

"A souvenir, maybe?" Lyons said.

"Not my area of expertise, Inspector. That's for you to figure out," Dodd said. He handed over a plastic bag with a small gold stud earring inside. There was a very small ruby-coloured piece of glass at the centre of the tiny jewel, surrounded by five small clear stones.

* * *

Back at the Garda station Lyons gathered her diminished team around her.

"Right. Plans for the day. Listen up everybody. Dermot – can you contact all the hotels in the Clifden area and see if there has been a John Hughes staying at any of them? He'd hardly bother with two aliases, and he might have to show his driving license to authenticate any booking he was making. Sally – you and me are going out west. I want to talk to that Carol girl again, and then I want us to go and see the Finnegans. I'd like us to go through the girl's room – see if there's anything there. John – will you do some more work on this Hughes bloke? See if we can get anything more from the car hire company. Have we anything with his fingerprints on it?"

"No, boss, nothing," O'Connor said.

"Terrific. Right, let's get to it, the day is half gone already, chop-chop."

Lyons knew she was being a bit rough with the team, but for all she knew at this point there was a killer on the loose somewhere in the county, and he could strike again at any moment.

* * *

The Galway County Council offices in Clifden had recently moved to new premises over the large supermarket at the bottom of Market Street. The entrance was at the side of the building via an anonymous looking door protected by an electronic entry system. Fahy pressed the bell and after a moment a voice in the device said simply, "Yes?"

Fahy introduced them and the door buzzed loudly. At the top of the stairs, there was another door marked Reception, and the two detectives entered into a small vestibule where a girl was seated behind a rather cluttered desk. Evidently the council's budget hadn't stretched to new furniture when they moved location, as the desk had clearly seen better days. Its green vinyl top was torn in one or two places, and the modesty panel protecting the occupant's legs from view was displaying raw chipboard where the thin veneer had broken off.

"We'd like to see the manager, please," Fahy said, smiling at the rather sullen girl.

"Yes, of course. If you could just wait here a minute, I'll tell him you're here," the girl said, getting up from her perch and disappearing through a door behind her.

A few minutes later, they were shown into an office where the manager sat behind a newer desk, at the front of which was a triangular shaped name plate announcing 'Mr James Cassidy, Manager'. Cassidy was tall and slim with a mop of untidy straw-coloured curls all over the top of his head. He had pale grey eyes, a long narrow face and full lips.

Lyons was surprised that Cassidy was dressed in a pullover and jeans. She had expected a suit, but, she supposed, this was the modern way.

"Come in, ladies, take a seat. Can I get you a tea or a coffee?" Cassidy said, "and don't mind that thing, it's Jim," he remarked, gesturing at the name plate.

"No thanks, Jim," Lyons said answering for both of them, "we're here to have a word about Sheena Finnegan, if that's OK?"

"Oh, yes. Terrible business. The girls are all dreadfully upset. Nothing like this has ever happened before. Sheena was very popular, you know. A lovely girl. And from such a good family too. I'm going out to see Mr and Mrs Finnegan later to express my condolences."

"Yes, it's very tragic. We are looking into her background to see if we can establish a motive for her death. May I ask what exactly Sheena did here at the council?" Lyons said.

"Well, she is just, or was, one of our administrators, so she dealt with all sorts. You know: correspondence, planning applications, various licenses, septic tank inspections, roadworks – all sorts of things really. Of course, she didn't have any decision-making powers – that's up to the councillors themselves and the various committees. But there's a fierce amount of paperwork in this job. Sometimes I think that's all we do."

"And was there anything bothering her lately that you are aware of, Jim?" Fahy asked.

"No, nothing. She was a good worker. Thorough, and relatively quick, although she was still learning the ropes in some of the more complex areas of the council's work."

"Have you been through her desk?" Fahy said.

"No – of course not. Why would I?"

"Well, you might have wanted to move her workload over to someone else, or check that she had nothing upcoming that would need to be re-scheduled," Fahy said.

"Look, detective, this is a small office and everyone knows what everyone else is doing, more or less. The other girls will have taken up the slack without me standing over them. This thing is bad enough without launching some kind of witch hunt too."

"Would you object if we took a look at Sheena's desk?" Lyons asked.

"Yes. I would. I can't think that what happened is in any way connected to her work – it's ridiculous. And I don't want the Gardaí rummaging through her stuff in plain sight, upsetting the other people out there. If you want to go through her things, you'd better get a warrant!"

Fahy and Lyons looked at each other and didn't speak for a minute to let the heat go out of the situation.

"That won't be necessary, Mr Cassidy, not for now at least. Thank you for your time, and once again, our condolences," Lyons said. They got up to leave.

Back out on the street, Fahy said to Lyons, "Touchy, our Mr Cassidy, isn't he?"

"Isn't he though. Is he just upset, or is there more to it?" Lyons said.

"Hmm, hard to tell. He's quite dishy though."

"Easy tiger. He's not in your league. You can do better than that."

"I wish!" Fahy said, and they both laughed.

Chapter Eight

It was time to put phase two into play.

Eoin cleaned off the tiny earring he had ripped from Sheena Finnegan's right ear lobe.

He wrapped it carefully in a piece of toilet paper and placed it deep in his jeans pocket. Leaving the mobile home, he scrambled across the rough terrain, trying hard not to get his feet wet in the many grassy puddles, and made it to the road a few minutes before the Clifden to Galway bus came along.

He boarded the bus and took a seat on the left-hand side, a third of the way down where there were few others seated around.

The bus made its way steadily across the undulating road towards the city.

As it approached Moycullen, Eoin spotted a Fiat Punto on the grass at the side of the road with a piece of white A4 paper in the windscreen offering the car for sale. It was an old red model, and the asking price, which was displayed in large black letters, was just €450.

Eoin stood up and asked the driver to let him out. He walked back to the house where the car was on offer, and knocked on the door.

Amazingly, he discovered that the car had a current tax disc and NCT certificate. After a bit of haggling, Eoin parted with €410 and drove away in the little car which he was even more surprised to find was three-quarters full of petrol. He couldn't believe his luck.

Eoin drove the car into the city and parked it in Hayne's Yard car park, undercover and out of sight.

He walked into the centre of the town and purchased a small padded envelope. He then went to the main Post Office, and making sure he was out of sight of the many CCTV cameras, he slipped the earring into the envelope; addressed it, and posted it.

He walked back to the car park, collecting a burger meal on the way from one of the take-aways in the narrow city streets. He ate the makeshift meal in the car, paid the parking fee, and left again, driving back out towards Clifden to his temporary dwelling.

Eoin parked the Punto out of sight in a derelict cowshed near to where the mobile home was located. No one would see it there. He trudged back to the caravan, satisfied that he had accomplished his mission – for the moment. For now, it was a waiting game.

Chapter Nine

When Lyons and Fahy had left the council offices, they drove out to Letterfrack to see Carol. The girl was busy at work, and said that her boss wouldn't take kindly to her spending a long time chatting to the Gardaí, so they promised to make it as quick as possible.

The three of them sat in the lounge of the hotel, in a quiet corner where no one could hear their conversation.

"Carol, I know this is upsetting for you, but we need to find out a bit more about Sheena," Fahy said.

"What do you need to know?" Carol asked rather nervously.

"Was there anything bothering her that she shared with you recently? Anything from work, or in her personal life that might have indicated she was in any kind of danger?" Lyons asked.

"No, nothing like that. She did mention something about some strange goings on in the office, but to be honest, I wasn't really listening to her," Carol said. The memory of her ignoring her friend brought her to tears, and she dabbed her eyes with a tissue, sobbing quietly.

"I'm sorry," Carol said tearfully.

Sally Fahy moved her chair across to be beside Carol, and put an arm around her shoulders.

"It's OK, Carol. Don't be upset. We're just trying to establish if her death was a random act, or if there was something more to it. Can you remember if she said any more about whatever it was at work?" Fahy said.

"No. I'm really sorry. I feel as if I have let her down. It's horrible."

"It's OK, really. You weren't to know what was going to happen. But can you remember if she mentioned anyone in particular from work connected with the strange goings on?"

"No. I don't think she named anyone, or if she did, I don't remember."

"Did she ever talk about Jim Cassidy?" Lyons asked.

"Oh, yes. She was always talking about him, Jim did this, or Jim said that to me. I think she secretly fancied him, but I don't think there was anything between them."

"Did she mention Jim in the context of the funny stuff?" Lyons said.

"No, nothing like that. Listen, I'd better get on with my work here. I don't want to lose my job. The boss is a bit of a stickler."

"OK. Sorry to have kept you, Carol. But listen – if you think of anything – anything at all, no matter how insignificant it might appear, please call me," Lyons said, and handed the girl a card with her details on it.

When Lyons and Fahy got outside, Fahy said, "Well, what do you think? Does she know anything useful?"

"I don't really believe she does. She probably got fed up with Sheena blathering on about Jim all the time and kind of tuned out. Still, we'd better check to see where Mr Cassidy was at the time the girl was being murdered. I'll get Seán to send someone round so as not to spook him, just in case."

"Good idea."

* * *

When Lyons and Fahy rang the doorbell at the Finnegans' house, it was answered by a young man in his late twenties. The lad was Sheena's brother who had come home from Dublin – where he worked for an IT company – to be with his parents.

When the introductions had been made, Lyons asked him if it would be OK if they had a look around Sheena's bedroom. He didn't have an issue with that, and directed the two detectives to a room on the right down the corridor.

Sheena's bedroom was small, but very well organised. A single bed with a multi-coloured duvet cover was positioned along the wall at ninety degrees to the window that looked out to the back garden where the land rose up steeply behind the bungalow. A pale, pine wardrobe with a dressing table of sorts attached filled the other wall, with a pink velvet covered stool tucked in underneath allowing Sheena to do her makeup in the mirror above.

The walls were painted a non-descript shade of cream – not quite magnolia – but not far off. There was a single light fitting suspended from the centre of the ceiling with a pleated Chinese hat styled lampshade. Beside the bed there was a plain white night stand on which stood a lamp with a flexible stem, and a small black Casio alarm clock. The night stand had a drawer and a small cupboard beneath the top surface. A full row of soft toys, dominated by a large golden teddy bear, was placed all along the window sill looking out to the garden.

"You take the wardrobe, I'll do the bedside locker," Lyons said.

They donned vinyl gloves and set about a thorough search of the room. Lyons noticed that the drawer of the bedside locker wasn't fully closed. She removed it carefully and looked behind it. There, taped to the rear edge of the drawer was a USB memory key. It was very small and black in colour with the brand name Kingston in green writing on the flat side.

"Mmm – look what I found," Lyons said, holding up the tiny device like a trophy. Fahy came across to have a closer look.

"That's odd. That's just like the one I saw on James Cassidy's desk. Identical, in fact!"

"Really? I didn't spot that. Well done you," Lyons said.

"That's why they send two of us!"

"Did you find anything in the wardrobe?"

"Nothing much. Just a packet of condoms hidden at the back of her knicker drawer. I don't suppose mum and dad would be too understanding," Fahy said.

"No, I guess not."

"Right. Let's get this thing back to town and give John a crack at it."

* * *

It was after six by the time they got back into the city. The traffic had been brutal for the last few miles, and the rain had started again in earnest.

"Drop me off at the station, boss. I'll give the memory thingy to John. You get off home. You've had a long day," Fahy said.

"Thanks, Sally, I don't mind if I do. I'm exhausted. See you in the morning."

Lyons struggled on with the traffic out as far as Salthill, where she lived with Superintendent Mick Hays. They had moved in together a few years earlier, and had managed to make an unlikely arrangement work very well for both of them. Hays' boss, Chief Superintendent Finbarr Plunkett, wasn't too keen on the idea, but he was prepared to tolerate it, as long as it didn't interfere with their professional work, and so far, things had been going well.

When she got home, Hays who had arrived before her, had got together a meal for the two of them. He was a dab hand with pasta, and he had made a delicious platter with spaghetti, sun dried tomatoes, garlic, olive oil and small pieces of tender chicken. He had also opened a bottle of excellent Amarone to accompany the meal.

"Thanks, hun, you're a saint. I'm famished," she said, giving her partner a kiss on the lips.

"Give me two minutes to change out of my work clothes."

They ate the meal in silence. It was rounded off with some shop-bought Tiramisu that Hays had collected on his way home.

When they got to the coffee stage, Hays finally asked her, "So, how did things go today? Are you any further on?"

"No, absolutely not. Our killer seems to have just vanished. But there may be something iffy going on with the council. We found a little memory stick hidden in Sheena's bedroom. Sally left it in for John to work on, so we'll know more in the morning."

"Motive enough for murder?" Hays asked.

"Who knows. We'll have to wait and see what turns up. How did your day go?"

"Mostly the usual nonsense. They're talking about doing a crime prevention month in December to try and stop the low life stealing all the kiddies' presents while the parents are out getting pissed at the office party. Increased men on the beat; close observation on the known tea-leaves in the area; meetings with neighbourhood watch to sharpen their snooping, that sort of thing."

"Do you think it will do any good?" Lyons said.

"It could do. It's good PR to be seen to be doing something anyway. We'll get it featured on Galway Bay FM and get it in the papers. It might send some of the low-life into the next county to do their pillaging."

"You know, Superintendent Hays, you really have become quite cynical since you took on this new role. What happened to the skilful thief-catcher I fell for all those years ago?"

"I'm sorry. It's all this bloody paperwork. Daft spreadsheets that I'm quite sure nobody ever looks at that take days to prepare. Literally hundreds of bulletins a month from HQ mostly about stupid crap that has absolutely nothing to do with law and order. It just gets me down from time to time. I miss the operational side of things," Hays said.

"It's a shame, 'cos you're damn good at the operational stuff. Maybe I can get you a bit more involved in this case if it goes on a bit. You'd enjoy that."

Lyons had no idea just exactly how portentous her words would turn out to be.

Chapter Ten

Hays and Lyons were getting ready to leave the house the following morning. They had finished breakfast, and Lyons was just clearing away the dirty crockery when she heard the letterbox opening, followed by the sound of mail dropping onto the mat.

"I'll get it," Hays said as he descended the last two steps of the stairs.

"Maureen, love – could you bring me a pair of vinyl gloves?" he said, looking down at the small yellow padded envelope lying address side up on the floor.

"Here – what's up?" she said, handing him the gloves.

"Well, do you know anyone with handwriting like that?" he said, gesturing towards the envelope.

"Good job it landed face up, or I would have lifted it. It's addressed to you." Hays picked up the little yellow package and placed it into a clear plastic bag. "Better get it across to Sinéad Loughran – see what she can make of it."

Sinéad Loughran was the bright and bubbly girl who led a small team of forensic officers attached to the detective unit in Galway. Sinéad and Maureen were good friends, and when deep in the midst of some gruesome crime, they often went out together for a few drinks after work to ease the tension. Loughran was an excellent forensic scientist, and managed somehow to retain her sense of humour, even when dealing with the most horrendous crime scene, or other morbid evidence.

Lyons brought the plastic bag containing her morning mail delivery in to Loughran's office.

"Hi, Maureen. What has you out and about this early?" Loughran said, looking up from her bench where she had all sorts of strange artefacts spread out.

"Hi, Sinéad. This arrived at home earlier, and Mick thinks it may be connected to the case we're working on. Could you have a very careful look at it and see what you can find?" Lyons said, holding up the specimen for Loughran to see.

"Sure. Give it here. Was it delivered by An Post do you think?"

"Yes. Well, at least it arrived at the same time as the post usually does. It has a stamp and it appears to have been franked. Why do you ask?"

"Ah, it just means that it's been handled a lot. You know – the sorting office, the guy who collected it from wherever it was mailed, the delivery guy; so the outside will be of bugger all use to us. Let's hope the inside is more informative."

Loughran used tweezers to remove the padded envelope from the bag and placed it down on her bench. She put a clean sheet of paper over the top of it, and then pressed down hard on the envelope with the palm of her hand.

"Well, I don't think it's a bomb, anyway. Too flat. Let's see what's inside."

Working deftly with a surgeon's scalpel, she slit along the short side of the envelope away from where it had been sealed. She then squeezed the envelope on the long sides which caused it to gape open. She used the tweezers again, and gently removed the piece of toilet paper – laying it on the bench – and started slowly peeling back the layers.

"Voila! Have you lost an earring lately, Maureen?" Loughran asked.

"No, I haven't. But I know someone who has. Here, let me get a close-up photograph of it so we can compare it to the other one."

Lyons positioned her iPhone over the little gold earring and took several photographs.

"Thanks, Sinéad. Can you go over this entire lot with a fine-tooth comb? See if there's any usable trace evidence. Dr Dodd has the matching one, still attached to the dead girl we brought in the other day, I'm afraid."

"Charming! Hang on a sec though."

Loughran took the earring up using tweezers and placed it in a little glass dish. She then took the dish over to one of her microscopes, and adjusting the focus, looked down on the item, turning the dish around as she did so.

"These aren't just any cheap old tat. Unless I'm mistaken, the stones are rubies and diamonds, and the mounting is 22 carat gold. These would have cost a few hundred euro, that's for sure. Somebody loved her, whoever she is."

"Hmmm, interesting indeed. They could just have been a gift from her parents, but on the other hand, maybe not. The real question is, why was it sent to me?" Lyons said.

"Just another secret admirer, obviously," Loughran said mischievously.

"I don't think so, Sinéad. I'd rather not be the subject of this bastard's admiration, thank you very much. Look, I'd better get on. Let me know if you get anything useful from the package or the earring, won't you?"

"Yes, of course. See ya."

* * *

Lyons went back to her office at Mill Street. She had just sat down and was logging in to her PC when John O'Connor knocked on the door.

"John, come in. What's up?"

"Thanks, Inspector. I did some work on that memory stick that Sally left in last night. It contains a bunch of what look like planning files. You know, planning applications, decisions to grant permission or refusals, that sort of thing."

"Interesting. What sort of dates are we talking about? Are they recent?"

"They go back about two years, and some of them are current, with decisions still outstanding."

"What kind of applications are they? Houses, commercial?"

"Both. Some are for one-off housing out and about, mostly to the north of Clifden. Some are for extensions to premises, and there are a few retentions where people have completed their construction without permission and are looking for approval now."

"Is there any common thread that you can see going through them, John?"

"Not really. But several of them – like more than half – seem to have been submitted by the same firm of architects."

"And they are?"

"Jeremiah Breslin and Company. They have offices here in the city. Just around the corner, as it happens. I've seen their brass plate on the door on my way into work."

"Thanks, John. That's great. Will you just print out the documents and put them into date order – latest ones first – for me?"

"Yes, sure. I'll have them in half an hour for you."

When O'Connor had left the office, Lyons called Hays.

"Hi, Mick. Tell me, have you ever heard of Jeremiah Breslin and Company, architects here in town?"

"No, I don't think so, it doesn't ring a bell. Why?"

Lyons went on to explain what John O'Connor had discovered on the memory stick they had found at the back of the drawer in Sheena Finnegan's bedside locker.

"If you like I could give my old friend James McMahon a call and see what he knows about them. It's a pretty closed shop for architects in Galway. He's bound to have heard of them," Hays said.

"Thanks. That would be great. I'm not sure that there's anything to it, but I don't like loose ends. Catch you later."

* * *

Hays wasted no time in contacting James McMahon. He had encountered the architect some years previously during the investigation into a murder out on the old bog road between Roundstone and Clifden, and had remained in touch ever since. While Hays didn't rate McMahon among his closest friends, nevertheless he was a useful contact, and the two men got on well together when they met up.

"James. Sorry to disturb you at your work, it's Mick Hays here. How are things?"

"Ah, hello Mick. That's funny. I was just talking about you the other day. We've been asked to sponsor that crime prevention week thing you have coming up. What can I do for you?"

"Great, thanks for that. I'm calling about something else entirely though. Can I ask if you know a firm of architects here in Galway, Jeremiah Breslin and Company?"

"Yes, I do know them, or should I say, him. It's only really Jeremiah himself that runs the practice. Why do you ask?"

Hays noted that McMahon's tone had become somewhat guarded as soon as Breslin's name was mentioned.

"The name has come up in conjunction with an investigation we're involved in. Nasty business too. What do you know of him?" Hays said.

"Mick, have you got time for a quick cup of coffee? I'd rather not talk over the phone."

"Sure. I'll meet you in ten minutes in Darcy's. OK?"

"Yes, fine. See you there."

* * *

Ten minutes later, the two men were seated at the back of Darcy's Café over two cappuccinos.

"So, Mick, how's things? I bet you've had a good summer out on that little boat of yours?" McMahon said.

"Yeah, it's been great, though that 'little boat' as you call it is in dire need of some fairly extensive repairs. Those old wooden hulls need an awful lot of TLC. So, anyway, what's the story on yer man Breslin then?" Hays said.

"Nothing you could put your finger on. He does a lot of work out west, mostly with one-off houses and a few business premises. But he seems to be able to get permission for buildings that we wouldn't have a hope with. Even if there are a lot of objections, if Breslin has his name on the plans, the objections just seem to disappear. He's been responsible for some real horrors out around Clifden and beyond – 'Palazzo Gombeeny' as we would call them."

"But surely all the architects are well in with the planners, James?"

"I'm not saying we don't spread a few quid around on nice meals out, or the occasional weekend away for some of them, but that's as far as it goes these days. If you get a reputation for that kind of thing, you can suddenly find your more respectable corporate clients departing."

"But you think Breslin is at it?"

"Looks like it – but I never told you. He'll be cute about it too. No brown envelopes stuffed with tenners or anything. It'll be a lot subtler."

"I see. Do you know of any particular projects that look iffy?"

"A few – but I'm not saying. You're the detectives after all. But if you need a clue, drive out the Sky Road a bit and up near the highest point there's a monster with fantastic views out over the sea. It must be 5,000 square feet at least. Quite out of character with the rest of the construction in the area. How did you come across Jeremiah anyway?"

"Sorry, James, I can't really say. It's to do with a case we're looking into out at Ballyconneely. I don't think he's directly involved, but there may be some peripheral connection. We'll have to see."

"That'll be the young lass that was discovered in the sunken car. Nasty is right. Christ, I hope Jeremiah isn't involved in that. I don't like him much, but that's a bit extreme," McMahon said.

"Well, keep this conversation to yourself, James. It's a very tenuous link for now, and we don't want to start any rumours."

"You know me, Mick, the soul of discretion. But I'd love to know if you find anything on him. It could be very helpful for our business, though of course we'd never say anything libellous about a fellow practitioner!"

"Of course not. Listen, thanks for the coffee. We'll talk again."

"Cheers," McMahon said, and the two men left the café.

Chapter Eleven

Lyons was just about to call Séan Mulholland in Clifden to see how Jim Cassidy's alibi for the night of the murder checked out, when Sinéad Loughran put her head around the door.

"Got a minute, Maureen?" Loughran said.

"Sure, come in. Grab a seat. What's up?"

"Well. We've been doing a bit of work on that envelope you got in the post. It's quite interesting."

"Great. What have you got?"

"Well, it was posted in Galway at the central post office, the day before you received it. There's CCTV in the post office, but it's impossible to identify the sender from that – there's just too many comings and goings, and we don't have a time frame. But that's not all."

"Go on."

"We managed to recover some very small traces from the earring itself. No doubt some of them will belong to the girl, but there appears to be a few very small flakes of skin caught between the stones too, and they don't look the same. Plus, we got some faint grease marks from the tissue paper the earring was wrapped in," Loughran said.

"Can you get an ID from any of that?"

"Possibly, but it won't be quick. I've had to send most of it to Dublin. They have better equipment than I have, and they may be able to extract a DNA sample, but it will take a few days at least."

"Anything from the envelope?" Lyons said.

"Maybe. It was a self-seal number, so no saliva, and the stamp was a peel-and-stick too. But we did recover a hair from where the thing was folded over. It's quite short, so it could belong to the sender. That's gone to Dublin along with the other samples."

"Wow. You guys are amazing. What do you think the chances are of getting an identification from all that material?"

"I'd say about fifty-fifty. We'll know in a few days. Anything else cropped up here?"

Lyons told Sinéad about the files they had recovered from Sheena's bedroom, and the interview with Jim Cassidy at the council offices out in Clifden.

"Oh, and I heard the council are digging the car out of the sand too. Apparently, it didn't disappear altogether, and it was attracting souvenir hunters who could easily be injured exploring the wreck. There's a lot of sharp edges on it where the firemen cut the roof off," Loughran said.

"Interesting. Tell you what. Why don't we find out what mileage was on the car, and compare it to whatever records the car hire company have? It's not much, but it will tell us how far the killer drove around the area before he went on the beach."

"Good idea. I'll call them and get the reading."

When Loughran had left, Lyons placed the call to Clifden.

"Hi Séan, it's Maureen. Did anyone get a chance to check out Jim Cassidy's alibi for the night the girl was killed?"

"Hi, Maureen. Yes – Jim Dolan had a word with him. Let me see, he left a note here somewhere. Ah, yes, here it is. It seems Cassidy went home after work at around five, had a meal, and then went out later for a drink with some pals in the town. He was in McGuigan's – not the same bar that Sheena was drinking in with her mates. He said he was there from around nine-thirty to after eleven. Then he walked home," Mulholland said.

"Hmm. Well, I doubt if it was him anyway. Why would he go to all the trouble of hiring a car when he has one of his own? He wasn't to know it would get stuck in the sand. But I'm not finished with your Mr Cassidy just yet, Séan. We found some files stashed away in Sheena Finnegan's bedroom on a memory stick concerning planning. So, we'll be doing a bit more digging."

"Do you think they could be connected to the girl's death, Maureen?"

"Possibly, but as you know, I don't like loose ends."

"Fair enough. Let me know what you find," Mulholland said.

"Will do. Thanks."

* * *

Lyons was frustrated. She didn't like hanging around while they waited for the forensic lab in Dublin to get back about the DNA traces they may or may not have found on the tiny pieces that Sinéad Loughran had sent up to them.

She decided to pay a visit to Mr Jeremiah Breslin to see if she could find out anything about the planning files that Sheena had taken home with her.

"C'mon, Sally – let's get out of here before I go mad."

They walked around to the small side street where Jeremiah Breslin plied his dubious trade. His office was accessed by a slightly tired looking red door that opened onto the street. There was a brass plate screwed into the wall beside the door announcing his presence, but it was very tarnished, and hadn't seen a rub of Brasso in years. They found the door was not actually closed. It had swollen in the rain, and was standing slightly ajar, so they went in.

The entrance opened into a tiny narrow hallway with a stairway almost immediately in front of it. The walls were covered in woodchip wallpaper that had at one time been overpainted with magnolia emulsion, but the colour had been replaced with dirty stains where damp clothes had rubbed against it. A slimy grey carpet adorned the stairs, and the smell of must and damp pervaded the fetid air.

Lyons and Fahy climbed the stairs, arriving at a landing area with two doors, one of which had a battered sign for reception.

Fahy tried the door, but it was locked. She knocked firmly and waited, but there was no response. If Breslin had a receptionist, then she wasn't in attendance that day in any case.

Lyons tried the other door, but it too was locked, so they decided to leave. Just as they were emerging back out onto the street, a rather dishevelled looking individual in a crumpled brown suit and well-worn black shoes approached.

"Good day, ladies. How can I be of assistance?"

Breslin was not in good shape. He was overweight, and poorly groomed, with a small amount of greasy grey hair arranged in a combover across his largely bald pate. His shirt, also grey, had food stains on it, and his skin was blotchy and flushed around the face.

"And you are?" Lyons asked.

"Jeremiah Breslin, at your service." He gave a small bow in their direction.

"Oh, hello Mr Breslin. We were just coming to see you."

Lyons held up her warrant card, and the cheesy smile that Breslin had been exhibiting vanished to be replaced by a hostile scowl.

"Well, you'd better come in, I suppose."

The trio made their way back up the tatty staircase. Breslin used a single Yale key to open the door on the right-hand side of the landing, leading the way into a very untidy and disorganised office. The desk – an ageing veneered chipboard number – creaked with the weight of papers and books of various kinds, and the single bookcase was similarly overloaded with journals that looked to be almost as old as the man himself. The single window in the office was filthy, and the set of vertical blinds on the inside of it were broken, and lay scattered on the window sill below. There were two tubular steel and tweed chairs positioned in front of the desk that had seen better days, and Breslin struggled in behind it to sit on his own slightly more comfortable furniture, collapsing into the chair with a heavy sigh.

"Mr Breslin, we are investigating a serious incident that took place out near Clifden recently in which a young girl unfortunately lost her life. The full circumstances of her death are not yet clear to us, but we suspect foul play," Lyons said, playing down the seriousness of the matter.

"I'm sorry to hear that, Inspector – yes, I had heard something of those events. Very sad. But how can I help you?"

"Well, your name had cropped up in the course of our investigations. The girl worked for the council out there. She seemed to have an interest in the planning department," Lyons went on.

At this, Breslin visibly flinched, and began to fidget restlessly with his hands; he lost eye contact with Lyons.

"I see. I hope you're not suggesting that I might have had anything to do with it, are you?"

"Did you, Mr Breslin?" Fahy said.

"No, no of course not, and I resent the implication," he said, his face reddening with indignation.

"How well do you know the people in Clifden County Council, Mr Breslin?" Lyons said.

"I have quite a lot of dealings with them, as any architect worth his salt would have. Why do you ask?"

"Is there anyone in particular that you're close to out there?"

"No. It's just the normal business-like relationship that anyone would have. Look, what's all this about? I'm very busy today, and I need to get on," Breslin said.

"We'd like to have a list of the projects that you have worked on in, say, the last two years out in Connemara, Mr Breslin. We need the clients' names and details of the planning permissions granted," Lyons said.

"That's preposterous! These are private matters, and nothing to do with that silly girl getting herself killed, I can assure you."

"If you're refusing to co-operate, Mr Breslin, I can easily get a warrant. And then we'll be looking into your entire practice in fine detail. You know, bank accounts, tax returns; all that kind of thing. It would be much easier for you if you just gave us a list of what we asked for."

"Very well. But it will take me a day or two to prepare. I can't just drop everything, you know?"

"OK. I'll get someone to call around here tomorrow morning at eleven, and please don't keep us waiting any longer than that," Lyons said.

The meeting clearly over, Fahy and Lyons left the offices of Jeremiah Breslin, and were glad to get back out into the relatively fresh air of the street. When they were well away from the run-down premises, Fahy said to Lyons, "Shifty – definitely shifty!"

Chapter Twelve

The wind was getting up now, and it had started to rain. It was that fine rain that blew in from the Atlantic Ocean on the stiff south-westerly wind, the kind that could wet you through in minutes.

The girl had left school when she finished games at just after five. It had been dry then. She set off for home on her bicycle, but it was hard going, what with the wind in her face and the rain starting to soak her clothes. The thick clouds had brought on the dusk prematurely too. Still, it was only a couple of miles, and her mother would have the fire going and some homemade cakes ready for her when she got in.

As she wobbled along fighting the wind and the weather, Eoin pulled up beside her in his battered old Fiat Punto.

"Are you going far?" he asked in a friendly tone through the open window.

"No, not far. Just another mile or so," she said, bending down to answer the rather good-looking young man.

"It's a bad old night. Why don't we put the bike in the boot and I'll give you a lift? We'll only be a few minutes."

The girl had been warned time and time again about not taking lifts from strangers. But he looked so friendly, and the rain was really setting in quite hard now.

Eoin sensed her reluctance.

"Don't be worried. I work in the town. Everyone knows me," he said reassuringly.

"Sure, what harm? Right, thanks, but will the bike fit in the boot?" the girl said.

"You sit into the warmth of the car – let me look after that."

The girl opened the rather creaky passenger's door and sat into the car. It was warm and dry, not very clean, but she was glad to be out of the weather.

Eoin lifted the tailgate of the old car and man-handled the girl's bicycle into the boot none too carefully.

"Who cares," he said to himself, "she won't be needing it again anyway!"

When he sat into the driver's seat, he reached into the driver's door pocket and retrieved the cotton pad that he had placed there earlier. He swiftly shoved the pad over the girl's mouth and nose, holding it firmly in place with his right hand, while he put pressure on the back of her head with his left. Within a few seconds, she sagged lifelessly into the seat, her arms limp and her eyes closed.

O'Malley drove quickly to the old mobile home and stopped outside. He lifted the prone form of Triona Fox out of his car and carried her indoors. Once inside, he bound her ankles and wrists with strong duct tape, and put a piece over her mouth making sure she could still breathe. He used a stout chain to tether the girl to the frame of the structure, and placed her lying on the long settee under the front window which was virtually opaque with dirt.

He then went outside and moved the car to the shelter of the old ruin where no one would be able to see it.

* * *

Triona came around feeling groggy, and not really understanding what had happened to her. The last thing she remembered was getting into a car with a nice bloke who had offered her a lift home to keep her out of the rain. She had no idea where she was. The inside of the caravan was almost totally dark, the thick grey rain-laden clouds having brought on the night prematurely. She tried to move her arms and legs before realising that they were bound, and when she went to sit up, the chain restrained her movements, so that she had to remain supine. Fear began to wash over her. What was to be her fate? Would she be killed like the girl on the beach? Oh yes! She had heard all about that from her friends in school. And of course, the teenage girls had embellished the story so that by the time it had done the rounds, the poor unfortunate had been raped several times and had her throat slit from ear to ear by a raving madman.

Triona was cold too, and soon the tears began to flow. In her own mind she was doomed, and hoped that whatever happened to her, it wouldn't be too painful. She curled herself up into the foetal position and sobbed into the dirty cushions, filled with terror at what might become of her.

O'Malley peeled the tape away from the girl's face as gently as he could. He had already instructed her not to attempt to yell out, as no one would be able to hear her in any case, and he disliked screaming women intensely.

"What are you going to do to me?" she whimpered.

"Nothing, love. Nothing at all. I just need to keep you here for a while, so make yourself as comfortable as you can and you'll be fine. I've taken your mobile phone away and put it somewhere safe. Just don't try any tricks and you'll be grand. This will all be over soon. OK?"

"Was it you who killed that poor girl out at the beach?" she ventured.

"Of course not. What makes you say that?"

"Well, there are hardly two murdering monsters on the loose out here, are there?"

O'Malley stomped over to where Triona was lying and grabbed her roughly by the throat.

"Listen here, you little tart. Shut the fuck up now, do you hear? Any more of that nonsense, and I will have to deal with you. And don't think I wouldn't, bitch!" He released his grip on the girl before the red mist descended and he lost control.

Triona shrunk back onto the dirty cushions, realising that she had been very stupid to provoke him.

Chapter Thirteen

Sergeant Séan Mulholland was getting ready to call it a day at just after half past six. He should, by rights, keep the station open until eight o'clock, but in the off-season, there was little going on once evening came, and in any case, everyone knew that he could be found reading the paper over a couple of pints in Cusheen's Bar if the need arose.

He let the phone ring six times in the hope that it would stop, but when it showed no sign of letting up, he reluctantly answered it.

"Clifden Gardaí."

"Sergeant, it's Breda Fox here. I'm ringing about my daughter, Triona. She hasn't come home from school, and I'm worried sick."

"Ah now don't be worrying, Breda. She's probably stopped into a neighbour's place to get out of the rain. Have you phoned around?"

"Yes, of course. I've rung all her friends, and there's no sign of her. And her mobile seems to be turned off. They say she left the school at around five o'clock on her bike, and she was heading for home. She should have been here over an hour ago. What am I going to do?"

"Now, take it easy, Breda. These things always turn out to be something and nothing, wait till you see. Tell you what. I'll get Jim Dolan to take the car out along her route, and we'll probably find her safe and warm in one of the houses along the way. What kind of bicycle is it?"

"Eh, it's a girl's bike. Dark green with a black saddle and a basket on the front. You know, kind of old style."

"Right. Well you stay there for when she turns up, and let me know as soon as you can. I'll be in touch a bit later," Mulholland said.

"Thanks, Séan. It's not like her at all."

Mulholland didn't know if Mrs Fox had heard all about Sheena Finnegan, but in any case, this situation was not one he should let lie. Urgent action was needed, so he started putting the wheels in motion, working more quickly than his usual gentle pace.

Firstly, he contacted his own small team of men and instructed them to start a search for the girl. He asked Peadar Tobin to go out to the Fox's house and get a recent photo of her.

"Try not to panic the mother, Peadar. Just say it's routine in these cases, just so that we have an idea who we are looking for. Calm her down a bit. When you get the photo, bring it back here and make several copies on the printer and hand them out to everyone who's looking," Mulholland said.

Next, Mulholland called Pascal Brosnan in Roundstone and told him to get Fallon and himself out on the road stopping cars coming across the old bog road from Clifden and asking the occupants if they had seen a young schoolgirl, either on her own or in the company of someone else, anywhere about.

"I'll have a photograph of her in half an hour or so, and I'll get Peadar to send it to your phone. I don't know how these things work, but Peadar has a good handle on it."

While he was waiting for Tobin to come back to the station with the photo, he thought he had better call it in to Galway.

Lyons was just packing up her things, getting ready to leave the office, when the phone rang. Herself and Hays had planned a quiet night in, as there was a TV show they wanted to watch at nine o'clock. They would order a takeaway meal from their favourite Chinese restaurant just near their home in Salthill, and would crack open a nice bottle of red wine to accompany it.

"Ah, Maureen. I'm glad I caught you. It's Séan here," Mulholland said.

Mulholland went on to explain the distraught phone call he had taken from Breda Fox some twenty minutes earlier, and the measures he had already put in place to see if Triona could be found.

"Good man, Séan, that's a good start. What's the weather like out there now?"

"'Tis the same as it always is. Misty and windy, and there's a chill to it tonight that we haven't seen all summer. Why do you ask?"

"I was just thinking if the girl had a puncture on her bike or something, she might have gone into someone's house for help, or shelter. Have you checked?"

"I have. Jim Dolan and a few of the lads are out now knocking on doors. And Brosnan and Fallon have set up a checkpoint out near the Fox's house as well. Peadar has gone off to get a photo of the lass from her mother. I'll have that here in a few minutes, and I'll send it on to you. Do you think we're overreacting, Maureen?"

"Maybe. But better to be safe than sorry after that business at the beach. Look, I'm going to get as many Gardaí as I can from all the stations between Clifden and Westport on the alert. I'll have a word with Superintendent Hays as well, and if he thinks it warrants it, we'll send a couple of minibuses full of uniforms out to you. Can you co-ordinate things there?"

"Oh, I can to be sure. But maybe the poor girl is warm and dry having a cup of tea in one of the neighbours' homes. She'll be rightly embarrassed when she realises what a fuss she has caused," Mulholland said, trying to reassure himself.

"Let's hope so, Séan; let's hope so."

* * *

"Mick, it's me. Where are you?" Lyons said.

"I'm in the car on the way home. What about you?"

"I'm still at the station." She went on to describe the position about the missing schoolgirl to Hays.

"What do you think, Mick?"

"It's a tough one, Maureen. What's your instinct? You often have more of a feel for this kind of thing than I do."

"I don't like the sound of it. I was telling Séan we might send a few uniforms out to his to get a proper search underway," Lyons said.

"Well, strictly speaking, she isn't actually missing yet. At least not by the rule book. But feck that – if the girl's in trouble, we need to act quickly. Yes – send the lads out in the bus. The trouble is, it's a huge search area out there, and there are so many empty houses at this time of year – you're talking about a needle in a haystack."

When Lyons had finished the call, she had an idea. Hays would go mad if he knew what she was planning, but to hell with it. A girl's life could be at stake.

She looked up the phone number for the Shannon Air Sea Rescue service and made the call.

The phone was answered by the night duty man at Shannon. Lyons explained the situation to him, and said that if at all possible she would like them to launch their helicopter to scour the area around Clifden and Ballyconneely to identify houses that were occupied. That way the Gardaí could eliminate as much as ninety per cent of useless calls to lock-up-and-leave properties and focus their attention on those that had someone at home.

"Can I put you on hold for a moment, Inspector, I just need to check something," the duty man said.

A few moments later he was back on the line.

"Hi again. Look, I'm sorry, but we can't put the helicopter up at the moment. There's a low mist over the area you described, and the forecast isn't good either. It would be useless, and dangerous. I'm sorry. If you leave me your number, and if things change, I'll give you a call, OK?"

"Yes, thanks. It was a bit of a long shot anyway. Give me a call if it clears – anytime, right through the night."

As she finished the call, Lyons said to herself, "Well, at least I'll avoid a ticking off from someone about his precious budgets!"

Lyons was contemplating her next move when her phone pinged. She picked it up and saw that Séan Mulholland had sent a photograph of the missing girl. She was dressed in her school uniform of a white blouse and striped tie, with a round, fresh face and long dark brown hair parted at the top of her head flowing down over her shoulders. She was pretty, if not beautiful, and had a glint in her eye that spelled mischief and fun to Lyons.

Lyons stared at the image for a few moments.

"God, I hope no harm has come to you, Triona, you poor thing."

Then Lyons had another idea.

* * *

"Joe. Hello Joe. This is Inspector Lyons. How are you keeping?"

"Oh, hello Inspector. Good thanks, and you?"

"Fine thanks. And how is Brutus?"

"He's great. I've just been out for a nice long walk with him. I think he's a bit bored. He hasn't seen any action for a week or two."

Brutus was Joe Mason's magnificent dark sable Alsatian dog. He was highly trained, and loved working with the Gardaí. It had been Joe and Brutus that had found the dead body of a girl left behind after a botched kidnap at Dog's Bay a couple of years earlier. Lyons still remembered the total dedication of the pair to the task in hand, and the sad look in the dog's eyes when the corpse had been finally located in a half-built deserted cottage.

"Well, I just might have the answer to that, Joe." She went on to explain the missing schoolgirl.

"Could you meet me out at the school at the edge of Clifden – you know the one near the bridge on the Roundstone road?" Lyons said.

"Yes, sure. But Brutus will need some item of clothing, or something that she has handled, if he is going to be able to pick up the scent."

"Don't worry, I'll look after that. See you both in about forty minutes."

On the way out in the car, Lyons called Séan Mulholland again and told him that she had arranged to meet the dog handler at the gates of the school.

"They'll need an item of Triona's clothing for the dog, Séan. Can you sort that out?"

"No bother, Maureen. Mrs Fox gave Peadar the girl's overcoat to keep her warm when we find her. She left without it this morning, it seems."

"Great. Better than having to go back to the house and bother them again. How are they holding up?"

"Well, so far, not too bad. They can't believe she has actually come to any harm. She's a sensible girl apparently. But, of course, they are worried sick."

Lyons explained her conversation with the Shannon helicopter base as well, and advised Mulholland that there was a number of uniformed Gardaí on their way out to him, and he should see if he could lay on some sandwiches and hot drinks for them when they arrive.

"I'm going to meet Joe at the school gates, and see if Brutus can pick up a scent. Have you got the photograph in circulation, Séan?"

"I have that. Peadar made nearly fifty copies here on the station's printer before it ran out of ink, and we're getting them out now around the place. Listen, you know I said Mary Fallon and Pascal Brosnan were manning a checkpoint? Well, there's bugger all happening out there. With the weather the way it is, they haven't seen one vehicle in over half an hour. Do you think that's the best use of them?" Mulholland said.

"Hmmm. Perhaps not. Get Pascal to stay there and ask Mary to meet me at the school gates. I'll be there in about fifteen minutes. Ask her to collect the girl's coat on the way."

"Right. Have you a radio with you, Maureen? The mobile phone reception is pretty poor out that way."

"Yes, Séan, I have. I'll keep it on and you can use it to contact me if the phone isn't working. See ya."

* * *

When Lyons got out beyond Oughterard, and onto the flat part of the N59, the weather deteriorated noticeably. The mist had turned to a fine drizzle that was blowing almost horizontally across the barren landscape. Here and there, patches of denser fog lay in wait for the inattentive driver. She slowed her Volvo down to a respectable 60kph. The fog lights helping her to see just far enough ahead to avoid going off the road, or hitting one of the many sheep that grazed freely on the rugged heathland. Eventually, she reached the relative sanctuary of the outskirts of Clifden, where although it was still very wet, at least the fog had dispersed a little.

Lyons pulled the car into the large opening in front of the school gates and waited.

A few minutes later, she recognized Joe Mason's white van approaching, and flashed the car's headlights. Mason pulled in alongside and they both got out of the car.

"Hi, Joe. It's a bad old night out here. No time for a young girl to go missing," Lyons said.

"Hi, Inspector. You're right about that. Did you bring something for Brutus to use for the girl's scent?"

"Mary Fallon is on her way out with the girl's overcoat. That should do it. How is Brutus anyway?"

"Impatient. He knows it's game on now, and he's keen to get started. I'll just let him out for a few minutes to empty himself after the drive while we wait for Mary."

Joe let Brutus out from the back of the van. The dog walked around the slick tarmac area in front of the school and found a satisfactory place to do his business. Then he came back to where Mason and Lyons were huddled against the rain. Brutus seemed to recognise Lyons from their previous encounters, and licked her hand affectionately as she patted his head and stroked him behind his ears.

When Mary Fallon arrived, she handed Triona's coat to Joe and Brutus was soon burying his snout in the folds of the fabric, familiarising himself with the scent of the girl. Then it was clear the dog wanted to get on with it, and he started sniffing the ground, finally setting off in the direction of Ballyconneely.

Mason had a special lead arranged for Brutus that allowed the dog to go quite freely wherever his nose took him, but still ensured that his handler had control. They had decided that Lyons should follow Mason and Brutus at a slow pace in her car with the blue lights flashing to warn any motorists that were approaching to take care.

"Do the lights not put Brutus off?" she had asked Mason before they got started.

"Not a bit. In fact, I think he likes them. Makes him feel more important; or so it seems. He just loves to work."

Lyons was always intrigued by the bond between Joe and his dog. It was as if they thought as one being. She often observed the dog looking at Mason for instructions, or conveying a message to him, and it was clear that the handler understood everything that Brutus was doing and thinking very well. Lyons marvelled at the telepathic signals that went between them.

Mason and Brutus made slow progress out along the narrow, twisty road. It was clear that the scent the dog was following was feint – probably diluted by the rain. But he stuck with it, and after a mile the pair stopped at a small gravel layby on the left-hand side of the road. Brutus sniffed around all over the patch of loose stones and eventually came over to Joe and sat down, looking up at his master.

Lyons stopped the car and got out.

"That's it, I'm afraid. He's lost the scent now. Sorry."

"Don't be sorry. It gives us valuable information. It looks like this is where she was taken, and if you look closely on the loose stones," Lyons said, bending down with her torch switched on, "you can see where a narrow wheel has been dragged across here a little bit. I'd say that was her bicycle tyre, wouldn't you?"

"I see what you mean. Yes, probably. So, what should we do?" Mason said.

"You two can get off home for now. We may need you again tomorrow if we can narrow down a search area, but

I'm going to call things off for the night at this stage. There's no point in this weather, and we need everyone fresh for tomorrow. Thanks Joe, that was great."

"You're welcome, Inspector. Now, can we just have a lift back to the van?"

"Oh yes, of course, sorry, I wasn't thinking. Hop in."

Chapter Fourteen

Lyons stood the search teams down for the night and set off back to her home in Salthill. The weather had eased a little, and as she drove back towards the city the clouds were scurrying across a big yellow moon high in the sky. The bogland was illuminated as the clouds passed over it with an eerie light, which had a strange beauty all of its own.

Lyons slept in the spare room, conscious that things might develop during the night and she didn't want to keep disturbing her partner.

She eventually fell into a restless sleep at just after 2 a.m., only to be woken again by her phone at ten past four.

"Hello, Inspector. This is Shannon Air Sea Rescue. The weather has lifted a good bit now, and if you like we can put the chopper up for you?"

"Thanks for calling, Tom. No, it's OK thanks. We've stood down the search for the night. And in any case any occupied houses would have their lights out by now, so you wouldn't be able to identify them for us. But would it be OK if we called on you again – tomorrow maybe?"

"Yes, sure. As long as we don't have a rescue on, consider us to be at your disposal. Good night then."

* * *

By six-thirty all vestige of sleep had left her, so Lyons rose and prepared for the day ahead. She left the house at seven, with Hays still in bed, and went straight to the Garda Station in Mill Street.

"Good morning, Inspector," the desk sergeant greeted her as she entered the building.

"Hi, Dermot. Anything strange overnight?"

"Nah, just the usual nonsense. We have a couple of drunk and disorderly lads in the cells. They got into a fight in one of the pubs down at the docks in the small hours, but that's about it. Sergeant Fahy is upstairs."

"Thanks, I'll catch you later."

When she reached her office, Lyons saw that there was a small brown jiffy bag placed dead centre on her desk with "Insp Lyons" scrawled across the front. The writer's pen was obviously low on ink, as they had had to go over the name several times to make it legible.

Lyons called Sally Fahy in from the open plan.

"Hi Sally. Have you seen this?"

"Yes. I brought it up for you – the night man gave it to me when I came in. He said it just appeared under the front door at about five o'clock."

"Terrific. And no one thought to call me! Look, get the CCTV tape from the front of the building and see who deposited this. And get Sinéad over here as soon as possible. Tell her to bring her kit with her."

"Right, boss. Sorry, I didn't think."

Lyons placed a sheet of clean white paper over the jiffy bag to protect it from contamination, and pressed her right palm down gently on top of it. There was something rectangular and hard inside the envelope, so she waited till Sinéad Loughran arrived a few minutes later before going any further.

"Hi Maureen," Sinéad said cheerily as she entered the office, "someone's been sending you presents again, I see."

"Yeah, but this one's different. Here, see for yourself."

Loughran donned a pair of bright purple vinyl gloves and lifted the package gingerly off the desk.

"I see what you mean. Well, let's see what you've got this time," Loughran said reaching for her box of tricks.

Sinéad took a scalpel and working at the base of the jiffy bag, away from the seal, she gently sliced it open. Then, without disturbing the contents, she peered inside.

"Ooh look – a mobile phone. Are you due an upgrade?" Loughran said with a twinkle in her eye.

"Ha. Very funny. Anything else?"

"Yep. Hang on a sec."

She reached down into her kit box again and this time came up with long-nosed tweezers. She inserted the tool into the packet and withdrew a small piece of crumpled tissue paper that had been folded carefully in four. She placed the paper on the desk and gently opened it. Inside was a lock of dark brown hair.

"Jesus!" Lyons exclaimed.

"Quite," Loughran echoed.

Loughran retrieved a small plastic evidence bag and placed the lock of hair and the tissue paper inside, sealing it, and writing the date and time on the label.

"What about the phone?" Lyons asked.

"We'd better turn it on. There could be a message on it for you, or would you prefer if I gave it straight to John to see what he can get from it?" Loughran said.

"No. Dust it for prints first. Then we'll turn it on. Whoever sent it probably doesn't know that I get to work this early anyway," Lyons said.

"OK."

Loughran spread a clean sheet of paper out on Lyons' desk, and proceeded to dust the little black Nokia phone with her brush and grey fingerprint powder.

"Sorry, Maureen, nothing," she said, having turned it over and dusted it all around.

"OK. There may be something on the SIM card, but let's not go there yet. Turn it on."

Loughran pressed the tiny red power button on the phone. The familiar Nokia sound told them that the battery was at least alive, and after a moment or two the phone pinged indicating that there was a message.

"What does it say?" Lyons asked.

"'Await instructions'; that's it. And it's clearly a burner. The battery's only about a third full, so we'd better get a charger for it soon," Loughran said, turning the little screen around so that Lyons could see the message.

"I think I have an old one here that will fit," Lyons said rooting in her desk drawer.

"Yep, thought so. Give it here and I'll plug it in. Can you do something with that lock of hair?"

"Yeah, sure, but I'll need to get some of the missing girl's DNA for a comparison – or a few hairs, say, from her hair brush. Can you sort that for me?"

"I don't want to tell the mother about this development yet. I have the girl's overcoat in my car – we were using it with Joe Mason and Brutus last night to see if we could track her. There may be some hairs stuck in the fabric. Would that do?"

"Perfect. Give me your keys, and I'll go and get it. I'll let you know as soon as I have anything, and I'll leave the car keys at the front desk."

"Great, thanks. Oh, and by the way, have you anything on the other envelope – you know the first one that went to my home, and the earring?"

"No. Not yet, but we might have something later in the day. I'll follow it up as soon as I get back to the lab."

When Loughran had gone off to retrieve the girl's overcoat, Sally Fahy came back into Lyons' office.

"Hi, Sally. Did you get anything from the CCTV?"

"Very little, boss. Just some guy in a hoodie and black jeans pushing the envelope under the door. But no facial picture or anything else for that matter."

"Well, we should be able to tell something from it. Age? Build? The speed he was working at – all of that would give us some clues about him," Lyons said, rather frustrated at the junior officer's lack of observation.

"Oh, I see what you mean. Here – have a look at it on my laptop."

The two detectives studied the grainy black and white image from the CCTV that was permanently on at the front door of the Garda station.

"Well, he's quite young. What would you say – in his late twenties or early thirties?" Lyons said.

"Yeah, seems about right. And he's not overweight either, in fact I'd say he's probably a skinny guy."

"How do you know it's a guy?" Lyons said.

"By the way he walks away. Kind of a bit like a punk roll. No girl struts like that."

"Good. You're right. So, what have we? A bloke, late twenties or early thirties, slim, fit, fancies himself and wears a grey hoodie and black jeans with trainers. Shouldn't be too hard to find, eh?" Lyons said.

Fahy looked at Lyons for a moment, not quite sure how to take her last remark.

"Just kidding! God, I love winding you up!"

"Do you want me to put this out?" Fahy asked, pointing to the frozen image on the laptop's screen.

"Na. No point. But you could check to see if any other cameras in the area picked anything up. Get one of the uniforms on it. We can't spare you for that," Lyons said.

"What do we do now then?" Fahy asked.

"I'd like to get John in. See what he makes of our new acquisition here. He might have some ideas. Could you get him for me?"

"Yes, sure. Back in a mo."

Sally was back a minute later with John O'Connor.

"John, this thing arrived early this morning, hand delivered. I don't want to miss anything that comes in on it, but could you have a look at it and see what you make of it? You know – where it was bought, and how long ago. If there's any trace of it being used previously, or of course, any identification it might carry. But be careful with it – a girl's life may depend on it being in full working order."

"Yes, sure, boss. I'll be careful with it. Give me an hour or thereabouts and I'll get back to you." O'Connor picked up the little phone and took it off to his workbench where he would explore the device to see what information it could yield.

When she had the office to herself again, Lyons looked at her watch and saw that it was just after nine o'clock. She lifted the phone and dialled the number for Clifden Garda Station. After ten rings, Mulholland answered.

"Hi, Séan, it's Maureen."

"Hiya, Maureen, we're just opening up here. Any news?"

"No. That's why I'm calling you. We need to get the search underway again as soon as possible. Can you organise some volunteers from around the town, and get as many of your own men out as you can manage? I want every house in the area knocked up, and any sign of suspicious activity, no matter how insignificant it might appear, reported back to me immediately. Can you set up a few checkpoints as well, and make sure every driver is interviewed briefly to see if they have seen anything?"

"Right. I'll get working on that as soon as I can, but as you know, Maureen, things don't start as early out here as they do in the city. It will take a wee while for all that to be mobilized."

"Just remember, Séan, a young girl's life might depend on how quickly we find her, so don't hang about. OK?"

"Understood, Inspector. I'll get to it."

"Oh, and Séan, if you think a helicopter might help, Shannon are on stand-by."

"That could be handy, OK. Might help to flush the bugger out. Can you organise it from there?"

"Yes, I'll get someone onto it straight away. Tell your lot to keep an eye out for it."

Chapter Fifteen

Triona Fox had spent a very uncomfortable night. The man had left her alone, but she was still tethered to the caravan. She found it impossible to get into a comfy position. Her mind wouldn't stop racing either. She felt reasonably happy that he wasn't going to molest her – he would have done that already if it was going to happen, she thought – but what had he in mind to do with her? When she heard him stirring in the other part of the mobile home, she called out.

"Hey. Hey. I need to go to the loo," she called.

The door opened and Eoin came in.

"Right. C'mon then, let's be having you."

Eoin untied the chain that was keeping Triona immobile on the bed. He lifted her up and carried her to the little bathroom that contained a toilet, shower and fold-up wash basin.

"I need my hands free," she said to him as he closed the door.

"Oh no you don't. You'll figure something out!"

He closed the door smiling to himself.

When she had finished, she called to him again, and he lifted her into the front part of the mobile home, placing her in a seated position at the table.

"And what would madam like for breakfast? We have an extensive menu. You can have corn flakes or Weetabix."

"Whatever, I don't care."

"Weetabix it is then."

When the bowl of cereal had been placed in front of Triona, although her hands were still bound at the wrists, she was just about able to feed herself unaided without spilling the whole thing all over her clothes. Then she had an idea. If she could just manage to equip herself with some kind of rudimentary weapon, she might be able to inflict enough of an injury on her captor to make her escape, but nothing came to hand.

As she finished the bowl of Weetabix, she decided that she would have to do something.

Turning the spoon around, so that the sharper end was pointing outwards, she pushed herself upright and lunged across the table at Eoin, aiming for his left eye.

Eoin's reflexes were sharp, and he dodged the main thrust of her attack, but the spoon caught his cheek and scratched a long gash through the upper layers of skin, prompting the wound to ooze blood.

"Bitch!" Eoin screamed, and lashed out with the back of his hand, catching Triona right across her face. She fell back onto the seat sobbing involuntarily with the sting of his powerful smack.

"Right. You're going back in the bedroom, and I don't care how tight the chain is – you can rot there for all I care!"

He dragged the girl roughly out from behind the table, scratching her thigh on the metal framework as he did so. He then lifted her up and carried her to the bedroom where he threw her on the bed and tied her tightly onto the frame of her temporary prison.

"Any more crap out of you, and you'll get a hiding you won't forget in a hurry. Get it?" he shouted.

Triona nodded silently, the cool metal of the spoon that she had managed to slip up her sleeve reminding her that she still had a slim chance of escape.

Back at the front of the caravan Eoin turned on the identical twin of the phone he had sent to Lyons.

"Damn. No signal. Fuck it, I'll have to go and find some bloody reception," he said out loud, and left. He made sure to tie the door securely behind him.

Chapter Sixteen

"Got a moment, boss?" John O'Connor said as he put his head round the door of Lyons' office.

"Yes, sure, John, come in."

"OK, thanks. I've been working on this little phone," he said, sitting down at Lyons' desk and placing the phone back facing towards her. "I got the serial number and called the distributer for Nokia in Dublin. This phone was supplied to a shop in Cross Street here in Galway three months ago. It was part of a consignment of two dozen very basic phones that are apparently coming back into fashion, especially with older folks," O'Connor said.

"Right, but how does that help us?"

"Then I got onto the shop. The girl behind the counter remembers the sale, because the person who bought that one actually bought two of the same phones and two SIM cards, which she said is very unusual. He paid cash too, which is even more unusual."

"Excellent. I don't suppose there's any CCTV in the place?" Lyons said.

"Well, there is, actually. But there's more. The girl said that as soon as the customer had got the phones, he loaded up the SIM card into one of them and made a call. She remembered this, because that too was slightly unusual behaviour. She heard him saying to whoever he called 'this is Eoin', but that's all she heard. He was giving her hard stares at that point, so she backed off."

"Wow. That's cool. So, his first name is Eoin. Ring any bells?"

"Not immediately, but I can have a look in the database and see if anything familiar pops up," O'Connor said.

"Who's getting the CCTV from the shop? Oh, and get onto the airtime provider that went with the phones too, and see who that call was made to."

"Right, boss. I'll get Dermot to go down and retrieve the CCTV and I'll let you know when we have more."

When O'Connor had left her office, Lyons spent some time thinking about what he had told her. She felt that the name he had given her stirred a faint memory somewhere in her head, but try as she would, she couldn't place it.

She took a page from her jotter, and doodled on it.

She put the words 'Eoin'; 'beach'; 'phone'; 'home address'; 'schoolgirl' and 'Ballyconneely' down on the paper arranged in a circle and tried to draw lines between them to make some sort of sensible connection, but she couldn't make it fit together.

"Damn it! There's something here I'm missing," she said to herself in frustration, before her thoughts were interrupted by her desk phone.

"Hi, Maureen, this is Sinéad. Look, can I pop over for a minute? I have some news."

"Sure. But you could just tell me," Lyons said, a little impatiently.

"See you in a jiffy," Loughran replied.

Lyons looked at the telephone receiver, puzzled, but she knew Sinéad well enough to realise that there was a reason for her somewhat odd behaviour.

While she was waiting for Loughran to come across from her laboratory, which was at the far side of the courtyard from the main Garda station, she put a call through to Clifden.

"Hi Séan. How are things out there? Any sign of anything?"

"Not a thing, Maureen. I have everyone I can lay my hands on out searching; knocking on doors and making a general nuisance of themselves. We have checkpoints up all over the place too – but so far nothing. There are volunteers from the town and the school out searching the bog as well. Anything at your end?"

"Maybe – but I'm not sure. I'll know more in an hour. Do you think you should get Joe out with his dog again?"

"That might be a good idea. It will look good anyway. The papers are all over this now, and I think it's going to be on the TV later as well," Mulholland said.

"Right, well, will you give Joe a call and tell him I said he was to get out there? And try to keep the lid on the press if you can. If it's those two feckers in the Qashqai you needn't hold back!"

"Right so, Maureen. God, this is a terrible thing altogether. I hope the wee lass is all right."

"So do I, Séan; so do I."

* * *

101

Sinéad Loughran bounced into Lyons' office carrying a plain manila folder.

"Hi, Maureen. Any chance of a coffee? You might need one too," she said.

"That bad, eh? Yeah, I'll get John to organise it."

When she had finished asking John O'Connor to arrange two coffees, she said to Loughran, "Well – what have you got that you couldn't share over the phone?"

"It's the DNA and hair sample we got from that little gift you received in the post. I had it fast-tracked in Dublin, and they came up with a match in the database."

"Go on – don't keep me in suspense!"

"It's Eoin O'Malley. Remember – the guy you arrested coming out of the TSB bank all those years ago when you were a rookie?"

"Jesus – are you serious? The little scrote! I thought he went away for a seven stretch," Lyons said.

"He did. But that was five years ago. He got out this July, and well, we kinda lost track of him, despite the fact that he's on parole. Are you OK, Maureen?"

"What? Oh, yes, fine. Just thinking. What's this all about, Sinéad? It's bloody weird."

"He's obviously gone to some lengths to track you down. I'd say he wants to get back at you for lifting him. Some of these scumbags just don't know when to quit."

"Yeah, but it's a bit extreme, isn't it? And why kill the girl? How's that going to help him get back at me?" Lyons said.

"Who knows how his twisted, perverted little mind works. And now he has this other girl – she could be in real danger, if she's still alive at all."

"You're right. We'd better get a move on. What's in the folder?"

"A decent mug shot, and just the results of the tests."

"Right, well, I'm going to call a team meeting. This changes things. We need to step up our activities – big time."

* * *

"Right guys, listen up." Lyons had pinned the photograph of Eoin O'Malley up on the board and drawn red lines to the dead girl Sheena Finnegan and the missing schoolgirl.

"We now have an ID for Sheena's killer, and we have a good idea that he's taken Triona Fox as well. But I don't want this information going outside this room for now – is that understood? He probably doesn't know yet that we're onto him, so we have just a tiny advantage which I want to preserve."

Lyons pointed to the photo of O'Malley.

"We need to do some research on this customer. What are his connections? Does he have any known associates in this area? Who did he rub shoulders with when he was inside? All that sort of thing. Sally, can you co-ordinate this and get me a report as soon as you can? John, anything more from the phones?"

"No, sorry, boss. I've given you all we've got so far. You'd better have it back," O'Connor said, picking up the phone from the desk and handing it over to Lyons who put it in her pocket.

"OK. Well, get onto the airtime supplier and see if you can get a locale for the text message I was sent. They should be able to tell you that at least. And if anyone gets anything – anything at all – I want to know at once. Clear?" Lyons said, trying not to let her frustration show.

Lyons left the room to a murmur of "yes boss" from the team.

She decided it was time to give Hays a call. Maybe if they pooled their collective brain power, they could get into O'Malley's head. Unfortunately, Hays was not available, so she left a message for him to call her as soon as he returned. She was pondering what would be best to do next, when the Nokia she had put in her pocket pinged. She opened the message and read, "Meet me at the old petrol station, Mannin Beg, at 5:30. Don't tell anyone. Come alone. No tricks if you want to see the girl alive."

Lyons went onto her office and closed the door. She had time to think this thing out before she needed to leave to keep the strange rendezvous. Should she call in the cavalry? Did O'Malley mean it when he said that he would kill again? What had he in mind when they met? All these questions went around and around in her head, but she could find no answers. As the afternoon wore on, she decided she would have to make her mind up and get on with it, despite her severe misgivings.

* * *

Séan Mulholland was, in an odd sort of way, enjoying the intense activity centred around his normally quiet Garda station in Clifden. He was a good co-ordinator, and he had a number of separate teams out searching for the missing girl, involving Gardaí from several nearby stations; volunteers from the town; and the local Civil Defence unit.

Things were so well organised that he decided he could afford to slip away down to Cusheen's Bar for a spot of lunch, and he might even treat himself to a pint of Guinness over soup and a sandwich. He'd only be half an hour or so, and he'd bring a mobile phone and a radio with him so that he could be contacted at short notice if anything came up.

Mulholland settled down at his usual seat beside the open turf fire, and was soon tucking into a hearty ham and cheese sandwich and a bowl of brown coloured soup, described by his host as "Brown Windsor". He felt the soup would hardly stand the test of the Trades Descriptions Act, but it was hot and thick – just what was needed on a late October day.

Sitting at the next table were two old timers from the area. They were small farmers who kept a few sheep out on the heathland surrounding the town, and had come into Clifden that day to see if they could negotiate the sale of some of their stock that had been fattened on the rough grass and heather over the summer, but would not survive the winter on the meagre pickings of the harsh terrain.

"Do you know, Shamie, I was out last night bringing back a ewe from O'Brien's field. And ye know that old caravan that he has abandoned up at the back? Well, I could swear I saw a dim light coming from it," one of the old men said.

"Ah, go on now, Fergal, you're imagining things. Sure, who'd be out in that old thing at this time of year? Wouldn't they freeze to death? Was there any sign of a car nearby?"

"No. No car. But the mist was fierce blowing in. Maybe I did imagine it," Fergal said.

"Did ye get the animal anyways?"

"Oh, I did. She was grand. The dog found her and brought her back for me."

Mulholland was so engrossed in the local paper reading all about the forthcoming GAA game between his beloved Galway team and very challenging opponents from Donegal, that he didn't hear the conversation between the two men. He finished his soup, sandwich and pint, and strolled back to the station where things were still pretty hectic, but there was no sign of any breakthrough concerning the missing girl.

Chapter Seventeen

"Sally, I have to go out for a bit. I have my phone with me, so keep me posted, won't you?" Lyons said.

"Yes, sure boss. Where are you off to?"

"Just a bit of private business. I'll be back later."

"OK. See you."

Lyons had timed it well. She drove out along the N59, and turned down onto the R341 towards Roundstone. The weather was grey and heavy, and there was a nasty chill in the air, made worse by the stiffening westerly breeze. It wouldn't be long before the rain came down.

When she got past Roundstone, going across the old bog road towards the Mannin turn-off, she was stopped by Mary Fallon at a checkpoint just beyond Dog's Bay. Lyons brought the Volvo to a halt and lowered the window.

"Oh, it's you, Inspector. Everything OK?" Fallon said.

"Yes, fine. All quiet here?"

"There's been quite a bit of traffic through – but nothing unusual," the young Garda said.

"Have you been checking all the cars thoroughly?"

"Yes, boss. I've looked in the boot of every one, or in the back if it was a van."

"Good girl. Well, keep up the good work," she said and drove on towards the meeting point.

As Lyons turned off the R341 down towards the Mannin peninsula, the rain started. It was just a few drops on the windscreen at first, but she knew that soon it would be lashing.

"What am I doing?" she asked herself. "I must be crazy!"

After almost a mile, she came to the site of the old petrol station. It occupied a large, flat open space at the side of the road. The remains of two very old pumps stood decaying on what had been a primitive forecourt. They were the kind that you could work by electricity, but if the power was out, a handle could be attached to the front of the thing, and you could pump the fuel up manually. One of the pumps had been for petrol and the other for "Derv" as it was called – a special kind of diesel that was tax free, as it was intended for agricultural use only. Perched on top of the old petrol pump was a broken white glass globe that had once sported the word "Caltex", a name consigned to the annals of history in the petrochemical world.

Sitting a good thirty meters behind the pumps there stood a small hut. It was brick built, and had at one time been whitewashed, but now the weather had worn away most of the paint, and it was a neglected streaky grey in colour. This small building had been where the owner was installed when the place had been functioning, and from there he had sold some basic provisions such as bread, milk, cigarettes, soft drinks and chocolate. There had been just enough local trade to make the enterprise viable, but when more people acquired cars, paradoxically, trade suffered, as they were inclined to drive into Ballyconneely or Clifden for their fuel and supplies where greater variety and better value awaited them.

Lyons pulled the Volvo onto the hardstanding and stopped the car some twenty metres short of the only other vehicle – a rather tatty looking Fiat Punto. She sat quietly in her car for a few minutes, listening intently for any sounds that might give away the presence of someone else in the vicinity, but heard nothing.

The rain had brought thick, heavy grey clouds down almost to ground level, so the evening had become prematurely darker than normal, making it difficult for Lyons to see into the other vehicle.

She removed the key from the ignition and put it in her pocket along with her own mobile phone and the little black Nokia that had been carrying the messages from O'Malley, and left her car. Keeping a good eye out all around her, she edged over to the passenger's side of the Fiat which was the nearest to her. Nothing moved or made any sound as she approached. The passenger's window was closed tight, and there was condensation on the inside of the glass, so she couldn't see inside. She took her small LED torch off her belt and shone it in through the window. There, with silver-grey duct tape across her mouth, was none other than Triona Fox.

Lyons opened the door. The girl immediately became animated, her big round eyes attempting to convey some sort of signal to Lyons, but all Lyons could do was to see how she could liberate the girl from her bindings, and check that she was not too badly hurt. As Lyons leant into the vehicle to start working to free Triona, O'Malley came around from the other side of the car where he had been crouching to avoid being seen, and grabbed Lyons from behind, holding a pad of anaesthetic chemical to her face.

Lyons wriggled and struggled at first, and managed to stamp good and hard on O'Malley's right foot, but the fumes soon overcame her, and she slumped to the ground at his feet, dead to the world.

O'Malley dragged her clear of the car by the collar of her jacket. He then reached into the Fiat and removed the duct tape from Triona's mouth. Next, he slit the tape binding her feet and hands, so that at last she had free movement, but nevertheless, she was very stiff and sore.

"Out!" he commanded.

"This is where it ends for you, dearie," he said roughly.

Triona didn't know if he was going to kill her or what was coming next. She staggered clear of the car, terror evident in her eyes, but O'Malley was quick to re-assure her.

"Don't worry. I'm not going to hurt you. You're free. Just give me ten minutes to get clear before you start shouting your head off. If you budge before I'm away, I'll come back for you – that's a promise. Got it?"

"Y-yes," she stuttered, the tape having made her mouth and lips swollen so she had difficulty speaking.

"How am I going to get home?" she said, feeling a bit braver now.

"Sit in the Inspector's car. After ten minutes you can start blowing the horn, and flashing the lights. Don't worry – they'll find you. Now scram. We're out of here."

O'Malley bundled the comatose form of Maureen Lyons into the passenger's seat of the Fiat and tied her up very tightly. He knew she was feisty, so he wasn't taking any chances. He took the Nokia, and Lyons' own phone out of her pockets, stamped on them roughly and threw them as far as he could in opposite directions into the bog. He then drove off as quickly as the ancient Fiat could manage, and within seconds was totally out of sight.

Triona Fox did as she was told. She sat into the warmth of Lyon's Volvo and did nothing for almost fifteen minutes. She didn't want O'Malley coming back to get her.

* * *

"Hi, Sally. It's Superintendent Hays here. Is Maureen around? She was looking for me earlier."

"Eh, no, sir, she's gone out I'm afraid," Fahy said.

"Oh. Where to?"

"I'm not sure. She didn't say. She just said it was some private business. I thought she might have gone to find you."

Alarm bells immediately began to ring in Hays' head. He knew his partner well enough to know that she was up to something – and it wasn't something good.

"No, I've been in a meeting for the past two hours. Look, could you ring around and see if anyone has seen her? She may be out in Clifden or something. Let me know."

Fahy called Clifden where Séan Mulholland assured her he hadn't seen Inspector Lyons, and wasn't expecting her. After a few more calls, she eventually got speaking to Mary Fallon who told Fahy that Lyons had passed through her checkpoint about an hour ago.

"Great, thanks, Mary. She didn't by any chance say where she was going, did she?" Fahy said.

"No, I'm afraid not. But she didn't seem to be in much of a hurry. She drove on towards Clifden."

"Thanks, Mary. If you see her again, call it in."

Fahy then informed Hays of the conversation she had had with Mary Fallon.

"Jesus! She's on a bloody solo run to save the girl. Meet you at the front door in five minutes, Sally. We're going out there!"

Chapter Eighteen

Triona was bamboozled by all the buttons and switches that she found in Lyon's Volvo. She knew there was probably a phone in the car, but she had no clue as to which set of buttons operated the thing.

She studied the array of switches and controls and then she tried pressing a few, and after a couple of attempts, the screen in the centre of the dashboard sprang to life looking like a desk telephone keypad. Triona dialled 112 and waited.

The signal in the Volvo's built in phone was stronger than most hand-held devices, so it quickly routed the call through to the Emergency Call Answering Service call centre in Ballyshannon.

"Emergency – which service do you require?" said a calm, male voice.

"Police, police. I've been kidnapped, and I don't know where I am. Help!" Triona blurted out. She started to cry, more from relief than distress, but it made her voice difficult to understand.

"I see, caller. I'm connecting you now, please stay on the line. Can I ask if you're injured?"

"No, no, well I'm a bit bashed up, but I'm OK. I just want to get home. Please ask someone to come and get me," she pleaded.

By this time the call had been routed to Clifden Gardaí. The ECAS operator had been able to establish which mast the call was coming from, and routed the emergency to the nearest Garda station.

Mulholland answered the call himself, and nearly passed out when he heard the voice of Triona Fox on the line.

"Now, Triona, it's important that you stay calm. We'll be along to get you in a few minutes, but I need to know where you are. What can you see around you?"

"I don't know. I was blindfolded coming here. But I think I'm at some sort of old petrol station. There are two broken down pumps and a shed. I'm really scared. What if he comes back for me?"

"Don't worry, Triona. We'll be with you in a few minutes. Now are you outside or what?"

"No. I'm sitting in the police woman's car – a Volvo. He took her instead of me. I hope he doesn't hurt her," Triona said.

"OK. Well now, you should be able to see a panel of buttons in between the driver's and passenger's seat at the front. Press the one marked 'Blue' and tell me what happens," Mulholland said.

"Wow. The whole place is lit up with flashing blue lights. This is cool."

"Right. Now leave them on for me. That'll help us to find you. I'll stay on the line, but I need to get someone moving in your direction. Can you hold on for a minute?"

"Yes. Yes, OK, I'll hold on."

Mulholland called Jim Dolan on the radio in his squad car.

"Jim, I think we've found the girl. It sounds like she's out at Mannin Beg at the old gas station there. Can you get out there pronto and see if you can find her. She says she's in Maureen Lyons' car."

"Right, Sarge, on our way. ETA six minutes," Dolan said. He switched on his siren and blue lights and accelerated to the fastest safe speed that the roads and the weather would accommodate.

"Now, Triona. What did you say about Inspector Lyons?" Mulholland said.

"He took her. They drove off in that nasty, smelly little Fiat of his."

"Did you by any chance get the number of the vehicle, Triona?" Mulholland said.

"Oh, God, no. I'm sorry. I never thought. I should have, shouldn't I?"

"Well, it would have been handy, but never mind. Have you any idea where they might be going, Triona?"

"No. But I was kept in an old mobile home after he kidnapped me. But I don't know where it is. I was blindfolded. But it's very remote. He told me I could scream as much as I liked and no one would hear."

"OK, thanks, Triona. When the squad car arrives, maybe you could give Garda Dolan a good description of the place? If that's where he has taken the inspector, any information would be helpful."

"I can see blue lights coming now. Is that them?"

"Yes, that will be them. You're safe now, Triona, well done. We'll have you home in no time."

* * *

When Sergeant Mulholland had hung up, he took a sheet of paper and did some calculations. He reckoned it was about twenty-five minutes since O'Malley had taken off with Lyons in the Fiat Punto. He'd be hard pressed to average more than thirty miles an hour in that thing, given the weather and the state of the roads, so by Mulholland's calculation, he could only be a maximum of twelve miles away from the petrol station at most. But Mulholland also reckoned that he had probably set up his bolthole nearer than that.

He got on the radio.

"All units. All units. Bring your checkpoints in to within fifteen miles of Mannin Beg. Be on the lookout for an old red Fiat Punto with male driver and female passenger – possibly in the back seat or in the boot. Passenger is Senior Inspector Maureen Lyons from Galway. Suspect is not thought to be armed, but exercise caution. He is known to be violent. Over."

When the mobile units had acknowledged his transmission, Séan Mulholland turned to the large Ordnance Survey map that he had pinned up on the wall behind his desk. He took a red whiteboard marker and drew a rough circle with a radius of fifteen miles from the old petrol station and shop at Mannin Beg. He stood back from the map and stared at it.

"Somewhere – somewhere in that circle, my lad. We'll get you yet."

One by one, the mobile units radioed into Clifden that they had now established their positions on the perimeter of Mulholland's red circle. There weren't many roads leading away from the area, so they were confident that O'Malley was still within the catchment zone.

"But what are you going to do with our lovely Maureen?" mused Mulholland.

* * *

At the door of the Garda station Hays threw his car keys to the girl and said, "Here, you drive. I'll be on the phone. And don't spare the horses!"

Sally Fahy had never driven a car as powerful as Hays' Audi A6 before, although she had been on the Garda advanced driving course, so she was very competent behind the wheel. She put on the sirens and the blue lights, and in what seemed like no time at all they had cut through the busy evening traffic around the city centre, and were heading out along the N59 towards Moycullen.

Hays started by calling Séan Mulholland in Clifden.

"Séan, it's Superintendent Hays. I hear this little gobshite has taken Maureen. Have you any clue where they might be?"

"Good evening, Superintendent. We're not sure, but we think they are probably in an empty mobile home within a fifteen-mile radius of Mannin. We have checkpoints on all the roads out of the area, and I think we can say they are contained within the cordon, sir."

"Feck it, Séan, that's seven hundred square miles! Surely you can narrow it down a bit more?"

"We're trying, sir. I've been on to Shannon, but they can't put the helicopter up just now. The weather is not good enough. But we're seeing if we can get any intelligence locally on empty mobile homes in the area where some activity has been spotted. We're doing our best."

Intelligence, Hays thought to himself – hmph!

Then Hays realised that he would have to make a call to his own boss, Chief Superintendent Finbarr Plunkett, to appraise him of the situation. He got through to Plunkett almost immediately.

Hays explained what was happening to the senior officer.

"Christ, Mick. That's a right old pickle she's getting herself into this time. Do you think you'll be able to sort it?"

"I sure hope so, chief. I'm not sure what O'Malley is after, but I have every faith in Maureen. She's got herself out of some pretty rough situations in the past," Hays said.

"Mick, do you think you're the right man to handle this? I mean, what with your involvement with her and all. I can easily get someone else to take it over if you'd prefer."

"Oh, God no. I need to do this. And don't worry, I can remain objective – at least till it's all over," Hays said.

"OK, as you will. What can I do to help? Do you need more men?" Plunkett said.

"I'll know more when we get to Clifden in about twenty minutes. Is it OK if I call you back then?"

"Sure, and Mick – be careful. We need a happy end to this mess. I haven't lost an officer yet in the line of duty."

"Yes, sir, I hear you."

* * *

When Hays got to the station in Clifden, he quickly took charge.

"Right, Séan, what have you organised?"

Séan Mulholland went on to describe the search parties he had sent out to scour the countryside for any sign of life in the empty mobile homes where O'Malley might have taken Lyons. He then went on to explain about the checkpoints they had set up on the roads. As it was now completely dark, Mulholland said that there was very little more they could do.

"Not good enough, Séan. This is Maureen Lyons we're talking about. Has anyone interviewed the girl – what's her name – Triona Fox?"

"No, sir. We thought after the trauma she had been through it was best to just let her get home to her parents. She had a pretty rough time. She thought he was going to kill her."

Hays turned to Sally Fahy.

"Sally, get Triona's address from someone and go out and interview the girl. I want to know everything there is to know about where she was held. You know – sounds, smells, what food and drink he had there – anything that could give us a clue to the location. Oh, and while you're at it, see what she can remember about the car. Every tiny detail could be useful. OK?"

"Yes, sir. If I find out anything significant, I'll call it in."

"Great – now off you go."

Chapter Nineteen

O'Malley's car bounced over the rough track leading to the mobile home. The motion shook Lyons from her chemically induced slumber. At first, she found it hard to focus, or even to remember where she was and what was happening, but the fog slowly cleared as the car pulled up in front of the dilapidated dwelling.

O'Malley stopped the car and turned off the headlights. He came around to the passenger's side and opened the door, untying Lyons, grabbing her by the collar, and hauling her out of the vehicle. He manhandled her roughly into the caravan, placed her on the long bench seat that ran under the front window, using a small torch so that he could see what he was doing. He tethered Lyons to the frame of the van with a chain going through her bound wrists, and then turned away to light one of the small candles he had laid out on the table.

"Right, Inspector Lyons. Now we need to have a little chat. So, I'm going to remove the tape from your mouth.

There's no point shouting or roaring – no one can hear you. Understood?"

Lyons nodded. She knew that there was no point screaming for help, and in any case, she had something quite different in mind for this particular client.

O'Malley removed the tape from Lyons' mouth. He wasn't rough with her, which surprised her, but it still stung badly as the glue on the tape pulled at the tender skin around her upper and lower lips. He was careful not to stand too close to her as he did so, in case she lashed out at him, or tried to bite him.

"Right, that's better," O'Malley said.

"Now, do you remember me at all, Inspector?"

"I do indeed." Lyons described the incident where she had been fortuitously on patrol outside the bank when he came running out with a supermarket bag full of cash and a sawn-off shotgun, only for her to trip him up and then arrest him.

"Seven years. Seven long years. Have you any idea what that's like – that place? In with the scum of the earth, locked up for almost 20 hours a day. Eating the shit they pretend is food."

"Well, you didn't serve seven years, did you? You got out in five," she said.

"That's because I was a good boy. And I spent every day – every single day – figuring out how I could get even with you. And now, here we are. Neat, isn't it?"

"Not really, no, it isn't neat at all. What are you planning to do with me?"

"Easy girl. There's no rush. All in good time. Now, are you hungry, or thirsty?"

"A bit I guess. What have you got?"

O'Malley got up from his chair and went across to the little kitchenette area which formed part of the lounge. He bent down and took a packet of sausages out of the fridge. He held up the packet of sausages and said, "How many of these do you think you can manage?"

"I'll split the packet with you – four each – OK?" she said.

As O'Malley busied himself firing up the stove and arranging the sausages in the frying pan, Lyons took advantage of his distraction with the cooking to study the place carefully. She was firmly attached to a vertical beam that made up the frame of the old mobile home where O'Malley had removed the decorative wall panel, and her wrists and ankles were firmly bound. But she had been in tight spots before, so she decided to bide her time and wait for an opportunity.

When the food was cooked, O'Malley handed her a plate with the four sausages sliding around in their own grease.

"I need some cutlery to eat these," she said.

"Use your fingers," he replied sharply.

They ate their rudimentary meal in silence, with Lyons occasionally glaring at her captor with contempt.

* * *

When they had finished their simple meal, Lyons again asked O'Malley what he intended to do with her.

"Nothing. Nothing at all. I'm just going to leave you here," he said.

"What do you expect me to do?" she asked.

"In the words of the famous Auric Goldfinger, Maureen, 'I expect you to die'. You see, this place is so remote no one will ever find you. I picked it for that very reason. They say you can last three days without water, and three weeks without food. So, in about three days, that will be the end of you. And good riddance. But just to make sure, I have a little surprise planned for you as well."

"What sort of surprise?"

"You'll see. I hope you like surprises," he said with an evil grin.

"You can't possibly hope to get away with this, you know? There's a whole army of Gardaí out looking for me at this very moment, and when you're caught, they won't be too gentle with you. Those fine boyish looks of yours won't last long!" Lyons said.

"Eh, I don't think you're really in a position to threaten me, Inspector, do you? And besides, as soon as I step outside that door," he said, gesturing towards the exit with a nod of his head, "Eoin O'Malley will cease to exist – pooof!"

Lyons tried another tack.

"I need to go to the toilet," she said.

"Too bad, Inspector, you'll just have to improvise, I'm afraid. I'm not falling for that one."

"So, what happened to the girl on the beach?" Lyons went on.

"Silly cow. She was well pissed when she got in the car. All lovey-dovey and kissy at first, but when we started to have a bit of fun she got all prudish. Girls shouldn't do that to a lad – especially one that's been cooped up in jail. No harm in telling you, I suppose. When she started to struggle to get away, I kinda lost it, and well, she ended up a bit dead. Served her right if you ask me."

"Charming! So, what are your plans?"

"You needn't worry about me, Inspector. If I were you, I'd be more concerned about myself. You see, you haven't got much longer to live. So, it might be time to start thinking about what comes next – if anything!"

"Just like that. You're prepared to commit a double murder without giving it a thought?"

"Not at all. I've thought about little else for the last several years. You know you really shouldn't have tripped me up that time when I was fleeing from the bank. I did five years inside, but you're going to lose your life over it. Was it really worth it?"

"I'm a cop. That's what we do. And when they catch up with you, you can expect to spend the rest of your life behind bars. The first five years was just a taster. And as you probably know, cop killers aren't exactly flavour of the month with the screws," Lyons said.

"I told you, don't worry about me. Now shut the fuck up! I'm fed up with your whinging."

Lyons could see that O'Malley was getting agitated. Should she provoke him, and hope to draw him closer to her when she might be able to land a blow to his head, or some other tender part of his anatomy? Or could it enrage him so that he finished her off there and then? She decided to stay quiet.

O'Malley worked quickly, gathering the few bits and pieces he had brought to the caravan into a back-pack. He donned a heavy leather jacket, and put on a pair of stout leather calf-length boots. He then checked Lyons' restraints to see that she was firmly attached to the mobile home, and that there was nothing within her reach that she could use to attempt to get herself free.

When he was satisfied that she was properly secured, he turned to her and said, "Right, well I'll be off then. Have fun!"

He disappeared out the door.

O'Malley walked back to where he had hidden the Fiat in the shelter of an old stone cow byre. When he got there, he put down the back-pack and set about the little car with a piece of scrap iron he found on the ground. He smashed the front windscreen and side windows, and then poured a bucketful of muddy water over the roof to make it look as if the car had been abandoned a long time ago.

Inside the old cowshed, O'Malley retrieved the Honda African Twin he had stored there during his preparations. It was a high bike, ideal for the kind of cross-country work he needed, but fast enough when it got out on the road.

When he had the bike out in the open, he propped it up on its stand. He went back into the ruin and removed a few stones from the outer wall. He took out a plastic zip-lock bag, opened it, withdrew the new passport and driving licence he had stashed there and examined them.

"Hello, Derek Drummond!" he said, admiring the forgeries that he had spent so much on in prison.

Finally, he located the red and white crash helmet that he had stashed in another part of the byre, put it on; strapped on his back-pack; mounted up; started the Honda and drove off.

Chapter Twenty

It didn't take Sally Fahy long to drive out to Breda Fox's bungalow. Breda's husband had died in a freak accident a few years back when his tractor turned over, pinning him beneath it. Breda was left with very little money, and just a few acres of poor land that stretched up behind the house. Her husband had been trying to drain it, and make it into something, but after he died, Breda just let it out for a small rental, and took a job in the town to try and make ends meet. Triona was one of two daughters that she was bringing up on her own. Triona was the eldest, and recently she had managed to get some work herself at the weekends so that her small bit of extra cash eased things a little for her mother.

Fahy rang the doorbell and waited on the step in the rain. After a moment, which seemed longer, she heard someone approaching from the other side, and Mrs Fox appeared.

Fahy introduced herself, and asked if she could come in.

"I suppose so," Breda Fox said opening the door a little bit further, "but if you're looking for Triona, I'm afraid she's asleep. She's had an awful scare, you know."

"Yes, I know, Mrs Fox; it was awful for her. But I presume you know that one of our female officers has been taken by the same man, and we are very concerned for her safety."

"Yes, Triona told me he did a kind of swap. I hope she'll be all right."

"Well, that's what I need to talk to Triona about. We think he may have taken Inspector Lyons to the same place where he was holding Triona, and we need every little detail we can get about it so that we can narrow the search."

Mrs Fox was about to protest when Triona came into the kitchen where the other two were seated at the table.

"I heard the doorbell. Is everything all right?"

Fahy was the first to speak, while Breda Fox looked anxiously at her daughter.

"Hi, Triona. How are you feeling? That's a nasty bruise you have on your face."

"Ah, it's not too bad, I guess. It looks worse than it feels. I'm still a bit sleepy, but I'm OK."

"Triona, if you're up to it, I need to ask you a few more questions about the place that you were kept in. Is that OK?"

"OK. But I can't tell you very much I'm afraid." Triona sat down at the table too, and Mrs Fox got up to make a pot of tea.

"Can you remember how far it was off the road? How long did it take him to drive to it once he left the tarred roads?" Fahy asked.

"Hmm, I can't really say. I was drugged when he took me, you see. But on the way back, I was just blindfolded, so I'd say it took about seven to ten minutes to get back to the road. The track was very bumpy, and his car was a wreck."

Fahy made a note in her notebook.

"Could you see any other caravans or buildings anywhere around the one you were kept in, Triona?"

"No, there was nothing around except an old ruined place about 200 metres away. But it was deserted, it had no roof or anything."

"What about sounds? Could you hear anything outside?"

"What sort of sounds?"

"Animals; vehicles; running water?"

"No, nothing. The place was eerily quiet. He didn't even have a radio or a TV."

"Did you get the impression that the place was lived in much?"

"How do you mean?"

"Well, was there a fresh sort of smell in it, or was it musty and damp?" Fahy said.

"Oh, right. Musty – very musty, and the furniture was in bits. The curtains were all torn and hanging down, and the outside was covered in green stuff. Oh, and the window in one of the bedrooms was broken. It was really draughty."

"OK, Triona, thanks; that's great. Anything else at all that you can remember? Did O'Malley talk about anything much, or what he was going to do?"

"No, hardly a word except to arrange the food and let me use the bathroom. Other than that, he was pretty quiet."

"OK. Thanks, Triona, you've been very helpful. Sorry to have disturbed you. I'll let you get back to sleep."

Breda Fox let Fahy out of the house, relieved to see the back of her. When Fahy had got back into Hays' car, she called him on the phone.

"Hi, Sally. What did you get?" Hays asked.

"Nothing really, boss. She didn't know anything about where the caravan was located. She just said it was quite a way off the road. And she couldn't give any more details."

"Damn! OK, Sally, never mind. You can come back in now."

* * *

When Sally Fahy got back to the Garda station in Clifden with Hays' car, night had set in properly. Hays knew it was dangerous for the search teams to be out on the bog in the dark, and he didn't want anyone to get injured. On the other hand, he was desperate to find Maureen, wherever she was. He didn't know if O'Malley had hurt her, or worse, and he felt so totally helpless.

"Seán, I think we'll have to stand down the search teams for the night. Keep the checkpoints on the road, but get the others back in. We don't want anyone getting hurt. We'll resume at first light, so get everyone to assemble here at eight o'clock."

"Right, sir. I'll see to it straight away. Where will you be staying?"

"I've checked into the Alcock and Brown. No point driving all the way back just to come out again early doors."

Mulholland wasn't sure if he should offer to go to dinner with the superintendent. Perhaps the man was expecting some hospitality, or maybe he would rather be left alone – he didn't know. In the end he decided to leave it, unless Hays himself brought it up.

* * *

Mary Fallon was still manning the checkpoint on the Roundstone road. She had arranged for Pascal Brosnan to take over from her at nine o'clock, when she would go and get a meal and some rest. She would then come back on at 2 a.m. if the checkpoint was still required, and stay there till morning.

She heard the motorbike coming long before its headlight pierced the misty gloom. As it approached, she stepped away from the car out into the road, waved her torch, and flagged it down.

"Good evening, sir. May I ask where you are coming from?" she said when the bike had stopped.

"I was in Clifden, and I'm going on to Galway," O'Malley said.

"Can I have your name, please?"

"Derek. Derek Drummond."

"Well, Derek, have you got your license on you please?"

"Yes, hold on. It's in my inside pocket."

O'Malley removed his gloves and fiddled with the layers of clothing he had put on to protect against the cold, damp weather, and finally produced the little plastic card.

Fallon examined the license which seemed to be in order.

"Thanks, sir. Can I ask why you came this way? It's not the most direct route into Galway."

"I just love riding the bike on the twisty roads. It's fun."

"OK. Well, be careful now. There are loose sheep on the road further on, and you could easily hit one in the mist. Off you go."

She handed O'Malley back his driving license and as he sped off towards the village, she made a note of his name and the registration number of his motorbike in her notebook. She had a slightly uneasy feeling about the guy, but couldn't put her finger on what it was. They had been told to look for an old red Fiat, after all, but still something was telling her that it wasn't quite right. After a few minutes, logic took over her thoughts, and she decided she was just being silly.

Chapter Twenty-One

Lyons heard the motorbike start up and depart a few minutes later. She waited until the noise of the thing had completely died down, and then waited another few minutes in case O'Malley came back.

He had left a tea light burning on the side counter that shed just enough light to allow Maureen to see a bit, although it wouldn't last much longer. She examined her situation and formulated a plan. The beam that she was tied to ran all the way up to the roof of the old mobile home. But the roof was leaky, and where the wood was anchored into the ceiling, she could see that it had rotted away a little. If she could just get the chain up to that part, she would be able to pull it through the soft rotten wood, and then at least she would be able to move around.

After a few minutes of twisting and turning, Lyons managed to stand up on the settee. It creaked ominously beneath her weight, and she hoped it wouldn't collapse under her. Finding the cross beams with her feet through the thin foam cushions, she raised her bound wrists up over her head, but she wasn't able to get high enough to reach the rotten part of the beam.

"Damn it, girl! You need to eat more spinach!" she muttered to herself.

Using her feet, she managed to get another two of the cushions piled up on the sofa, and then she rather precariously climbed up onto them, giving her a few inches of extra height. Holding her hands high above her head again, she engaged the chain with the soft wood up near the roof, and then leaned back. It was the only way she could get leverage, and she hoped that if the wood gave way, she would be able to stop herself falling backwards onto the floor. It was exhausting, but Lyons tugged and tugged at the chain and leant her entire body weight against the rotting wood, and with a loud crack the beam broke and her chain was released. Unfortunately, Lyons was unable to keep her balance, and she fell backwards, landing with a loud thud on the floor. With her hands still bound in front of her, she was unable to break the fall, and her head hit the floor hard causing her to black out.

Lyons had no idea how long she had been unconscious. She came to with a ferocious headache, lying awkwardly, half on her side. At least she could sense that there was no blood leaking from her head, although the candle had gone out, and the place was in pitch darkness. She slowly tried to get up, but with the lack of light and the bang on the head she was dizzy and disorientated. But she dared not remain there. After all, O'Malley had said he had left her a surprise, and she had no idea what the 'surprise' was or how much danger she was in.

She started by getting onto all fours. She remembered the layout of the place quite well, and decided if she could

133

get to the kitchen area, she might be able to find an implement to enable her to remove the tape binding her wrists. After a few minutes casting around unsuccessfully, she finally found the little fridge, above which she knew was a drawer for cutlery. Maybe O'Malley had left some in there. She managed to haul herself to her feet with the help of the furniture. She groped around until she found a drawer that opened, and to her delight, feeling awkwardly around, discovered that there was indeed a good selection of cutlery inside.

Fumbling around in the dark, she located a knife. She managed to get it to bear down on the tape in between her wrists, but it was agonising work and her fingers kept cramping up. The knife was quite blunt too, so it took an age for it to make any impression on the strong duct tape she had been bound with. But Lyons was no quitter. She slumped back to the floor with her back to the kitchen units, and slowly the knife began to do its job. It took her a good hour, and her fingers were in agony. Eventually she was able to pull the remaining tape apart, and her hands were at last free.

Lyons lay back, tired from all the effort and relieved at the same time that she was making progress. It didn't take her long to pull the tape from around her ankles, and apart from a lot of residue from the sticky stuff, she was finally liberated.

Now she could move around, but it was still pitch dark, and her head hurt badly from the fall.

She could see where the door was. A tiny amount of light was coming in through the glass from outside – not enough to see anything in the caravan, but enough to let her know where the exit was.

She decided to get out. She opened the door and stepped gingerly down onto the grass outside. She was surprised how dizzy she felt, and for a minute, she had to hold onto the door frame to steady herself.

"Damn this weather," she said to herself. She wondered if she should wait till dawn before trying to find her way to civilisation. She thought about it for a minute or two, but decided it was better to try and get away. At least she'd be doing something. She moved away from the old mobile home, and keeping it behind her, set off gingerly across the rocky, marshy ground. She had been moving forward for ten minutes or more when she tripped over a rock sticking up from the uneven ground. She pitched forward, and although she put her hands out to break the fall, she was unlucky. Someone had been cutting turf there, and Lyons fell into the deep hole left by the enterprise, twisting her ankle badly as she landed in a pool of dirty bog water. When she tried to stand up to see if she could clamber out of the trough, her ankle wouldn't support her, and she fell back with a splash into the cold, clammy mess.

"Damn it!" she said out loud, "can this get any fucking worse?"

* * *

Hays checked into his hotel. He asked the receptionist for some basic toiletries as he had come unequipped, and they gave him a washbag and a little kit with toothbrush, razor, toothpaste and a small tin of aerosol shaving foam.

After leaving the things up to his room which was warm and cosy, he went back downstairs and had a light meal in the bar. But he was very uneasy. Not only was one of his senior officers lost somewhere out in the relative wilderness, but this particular officer was his life partner too. He knew from previous experience that she could look after herself, but still, he was worried sick. He picked at the plate of quite delicious food the hotel had prepared, and struggled to finish the pint of Guinness he had asked for as an accompaniment.

"This is no use. I can't just sit on my hands," he said to himself, "I'll have to do something!"

Hays paid for the meal and left the hotel. At least he'd had the good sense to bring his winter weight coat with him, and he needed it. The night had brought a sharp drop in temperature, and the wind had got up even more. It wasn't a nice night to be out and about.

When he got into his car, he couldn't decide which way to go. His emotions were struggling with the years of logic that his training as a police officer had taught him, and he wasn't sure which was winning. He sat there as the engine warmed up and the heater began to blow luke-warm air into his face and over his feet. He put the car in gear and moved off. He drove out towards Ballyconneely, and took the right turn after Keogh's shop down to Mannin Beg. He stopped the car on the forecourt of the old deserted petrol station and turned off the lights and the engine and sat there, thinking.

Hays thought out loud, "If I was Eoin O'Malley, and I had captured the Garda who had put me away for seven years, where would I be likely to take her? What direction? How far? It's not likely to be somewhere out in the open, nor anywhere that anyone would be likely to see what was going on, so it must be down one of the many old cart tracks that criss-cross the bog."

He decided he would spend his time exploring every single one of them, even if it took all night, to see if he could find Maureen.

He brought Google Maps up on the LCD display in the car and zoomed it right in as far as it would go. This revealed many of the tracks that he would need to check out, although there could be some more that were too old or too small to have made it onto the map.

It was painstaking work. He had to drive slowly due to the roughness of the terrain, and from time to time he could feel the suspension of the Audi bottoming on a stone. He hoped the sump wouldn't get punctured and bring his efforts to an abrupt halt.

It was almost 2 a.m. and Hays was on the tenth tiny track, bumping over the rough ground with the headlights of the car bouncing all over the place, when he thought he saw something up ahead. As he drove on, the dark shape of a mobile home came into view, with its back to a dry stone wall. Hays pulled the car up in front of it leaving the car's headlights shining in through the open door which was swaying in the wind. He got out, and looked around for some sort of weapon, in case O'Malley was still there and came at him. He found a stout piece of dead hawthorn lying nearby, and taking his powerful hand lamp from the boot of the car he advanced on the mobile home. He shone the lamp inside, and saw the discarded chain and scraps of duct tape on the floor. He climbed in, and shone the bright torch all around. The place was empty, and he was pleased to see that there was no blood anywhere to be seen.

Having established that it was deserted, he went back outside and shone the powerful lamp around in an arc, but could see no one or anything of interest.

Lyons saw the beam of the lamp passing by overhead like the light from a lighthouse. She called out as loudly as she could, but her cries were carried away on the wind, and Hays heard nothing. Furiously, Lyons scrabbled about at the bottom of the trap she had fallen into for a rock or anything she could throw out to attract attention, but found nothing, only the dirty rancid water. Then she heard the car start up and drive away again, and she collapsed back down into the dirty water and cried.

Hays decided not to call the cavalry out at that hour of the night. It was too dangerous, and it would be better to leave it to the morning when everyone had had a night's sleep. Then he would get the entire team combing out the area. He would get Joe Mason and Brutus out as well. The dog should be able to follow the scent from the van, and maybe even locate Maureen and O'Malley.

Chapter Twenty-Two

At six o'clock the following morning, after a fitful few hours' sleep, Hays started to ring around. Firstly, he called Mill Street and asked Sergeant O'Toole, the night man, to get Joe Mason and his dog out, and to rendezvous at Clifden Garda Station by eight at the latest. Then he called Sinéad Loughran on her mobile phone. She answered sleepily, and Hays gave her the same instructions, asking her to bring a full forensic team out to Clifden to do a thorough inspection of a crime scene.

By seven, the hotel produced a breakfast which Hays managed to consume with some enthusiasm, after which he checked out and made his way to the Garda station where Séan Mulholland was just opening up.

"Morning, Séan. Thank God it's a bit better weather today," Hays said.

"Ah, it won't last long, don't worry. It will be chucking it down by lunch time, wait till you see."

"Full of cheer, as always, Séan!"

"Well now, Superintendent, when you've worked out here as long as I have, you get to know the weather pretty well. There'll be heavy showers coming in off the Atlantic later. But the morning should be fine, at least."

Hays went on to fill Séan Mulholland in on the resources he had summoned from Galway.

"When they get here, I want everyone out at that old mobile home. There must be some good clues left around there," Hays said to Mulholland who was filling the kettle in preparation for the morning cup of tea.

Sinéad Loughran and her team of two forensic officers arrived at just about the same time as Joe Mason in his white van. Brutus was, as always, keen to work, and he was eagerly awaiting being released from his cage and getting going.

Hays brought them into the Garda station and addressed the group which by now included Peadar Tobin and Jim Dolan and several other junior, uniformed Gardaí.

"Right everyone, listen up," Hays said.

"I want the checkpoints manned again today. You know what we're looking for. Every vehicle is to be stopped and inspected, including the boot, or the back if it's a van. If you're in any doubt about the occupants, call it in and keep them at the checkpoint till backup arrives. Sinéad, I want you out at the mobile home. I'll come with you to show you where exactly it's located, and Joe, you can come too. Brutus might just be able to pick up a scent and point us in the right direction. Right, let's get to it!"

Just as the group were breaking up, the phone on Mulholland's desk rang. It was Pascal Brosnan from Roundstone.

"Hello, Seán. Is Superintendent Hays there by any chance?"

Mulholland handed the phone to Hays saying, "It's for you. It's Pascal from Roundstone."

"Superintendent, I was just going through Mary's notebook from the checkpoint last night. She stopped a lad on a motorbike here fairly late on. Derek Drummond was his name. She took a note of the bike's registration number too. Thing is, there's no such number. It was completely made up. And his license was fake as well. Mary took the serial number off it, and it's way out of range."

"Hmm, I see. I take it this fella was on his own?"

"Yes, he was."

"Which direction did he come from?"

"He was coming from Clifden. He told Mary he was headed for Galway," Brosnan said.

"Hmmm, OK. Sounds as if he is of interest to us. Put out an alert for him, will you?"

"Yes, sure, sir. Anything else we should be doing here?"

"Just keep the checkpoint manned at all times. And watch out for an old Fiat Punto. Don't let it slip through under any circumstances."

"Right, sir, will do."

* * *

Loughran's 4x4 followed Hays' Audi out the Ballyconneely road and then down the dirt track that led to the mobile home. Joe Mason brought up the rear in his van, bouncing over the rough ground. They pulled the vehicles up short of the caravan in case there was any forensic evidence that could be disturbed by the cars.

The door of the old caravan was open and flapping in the breeze, an old grey piece of net curtain hanging on the inside. It looked deserted, but nevertheless they approached it with caution. Hays went in front and called out, "Hello! Hello! Is anyone there?" but there was no response. He approached the door from the side and slowly poked his head around the door jamb. It looked as if the place was deserted, but Hays was taking no chances. He stepped up into the old mobile home, and went down the back where two flimsy doors divided off the bedrooms. He stood back from each in turn, and poked them open. The bedrooms were empty, with bare mattresses on each of the beds, stained and discoloured; the smell of must and damp was overpowering. Coming back into the main part of the home, he felt the top of the stove. It was cold. He opened the little fridge under the sink and saw that it contained a carton of milk, which was still fresh, and three eggs in a box that had once contained six. He then went to the front of the caravan and examined the frame which had been snapped off near the ceiling. A stout chain lay on the dirty settee that ran along under the window.

He went back to the open door, and shouted, "All clear. No one about."

He left the old structure, walking back towards his car.

While Loughran and her team started work on the mobile home, Joe Mason let Brutus out of his cage. Brutus trotted over to the side of the caravan and almost at once, the dog started sniffing up and down its length at the base where it was open, and started barking. Brutus was scampering up and down, then turning and looking at Joe and barking loudly, almost frantically. It didn't take Joe long to read the signals.

"Jesus! He's found explosives!" Joe shouted.

"Get everyone out, now! Hurry – the thing is booby trapped!" he yelled.

He reeled in Brutus' lead, and brought the dog to his side, stroking his head to calm him down and reassure him.

Hays ran towards the door, shouting at Sinéad Loughran to get out, and the white suited forensic team exited quickly, one after another.

"Get back. Clear the area. A hundred metres at least. Joe – come away now, and thanks. Brutus may just have saved lives here," Hays said.

He walked back to his own car and called Séan Mulholland instructing him to get the army bomb disposal team out. This was turning out to be a right mess.

When they had regrouped, Hays walked over to Joe and patted Brutus on the head, stroking the dog behind the ears.

"Joe, while you're here, take this scarf that belongs to Maureen and see if the dog can pick up anything."

"Right, sir. Give it here."

Mason took the scarf and rubbed it into the dog's muzzle. Brutus made a quiet grunting noise, and immediately put his snout to the ground, walking around in increasingly wide circles. Then he seemed to lock onto something and headed off in one direction, all the while sniffing the rough terrain. Brutus appeared to be following a definite scent, and a few minutes later when he had gone about four hundred metres from the caravan, he stopped at the edge of a turf pit and started barking again.

Lyons, who had dozed off after a most uncomfortable night, was woken by the dog, and looked up to see Brutus' face peering over the edge of the pit, which caused her to immediately burst into tears.

Brutus had more sense than to try and climb down into the hole. He pranced up and down excitedly at the edge of the opening, whimpering and barking. The animal knew that this would get his handler to come to his side quickly, and soon Joe was also looking down on the beleaguered inspector.

Joe let out a roar. "Here, over here! Quickly, bring some rope. It's Inspector Lyons. Hurry!"

Hays ran as fast as his legs and the rough ground would allow, to the place where Joe and his trusty hound were standing. Brutus was whimpering now, probably in sympathy with Lyons, recognising that she shouldn't be down in that bog hole almost up to her knees in filthy brown water.

It took Hays and two of the forensic guys to pull Lyons up out of the bog. She wasn't able to help much, as her ankle was badly sprained, and now swollen to twice its normal size. When she was free, and wrapped in a thermal blanket provided by Loughran, Hays helped her over to his car and put her gently into the front passenger's seat.

"Thank God you're OK, love. I was worried sick. I thought he was going to bump you off," Hays said.

"Huh – not likely. He's a lightweight. But a clever one, that I'll give him."

"Right. Well, let's get you off to hospital. You need to be checked over and get out of those wet clothes."

As Hays walked around the front of the car to get in, there was a dull thump that shook the sodden ground under foot, and the mobile home burst into flames. Within seconds it was engulfed, the fire being helped along by all the plastics and polyurethane furnishings.

"Shit! Thank God Brutus spotted that. Otherwise Sinéad and her crew would have been toast," Hays said.

"It's worse than that! That was meant for me! He told me he had left me a surprise – dirty fecker. C'mon, let's get out of here. I'm starving!" Lyons said.

"Christ, Maureen, you've really pissed this guy off. We need to catch him before he has a chance to get to you again. Anyway, at least the girl is safe. And that's down to you," Hays said, patting her knee affectionately, "but promise me you won't go off on one like that again without informing your team. That was a bit reckless."

"I promise," she said, snuggling in to Hays, but not meaning a word of it.

Hays drove Lyons to the small hospital in Clifden where she received immediate medical attention. Two hours later, she had had her ankle strapped up, been put into a hospital nightdress and dressing gown, been given slippers, and was fed. She looked a lot better. Her own clothes had been taken away, laundered and dried too. They were folded neatly on the chair beside her bed.

Chapter Twenty-Three

Hays left Lyons in the excellent care of the hospital, and drove back out to the scene. He had asked her before he left if O'Malley had ever mentioned someone by the name of Derek Drummond, but Lyons said that he hadn't.

Back at the now burnt out mobile home, things were hectic. The civil defence had arrived, rather too late to be of any real use, but they were scanning the rest of the area for any more explosives. They had doused the fire down so that now all that was left was a smouldering heap of charred metal and wood.

Brutus was lying down beside Joe Mason's van. The dog was looking very pleased with himself, and Joe had rewarded him with some edible treats.

Sinéad Loughran had located the old Fiat in the ruins of the cow byre, and was going over it carefully. She had found traces of both Triona and Lyons in the car, and had recovered Triona's bicycle which O'Malley had thrown away. It was a bit scratched, and the chain had come off, but Sinéad reckoned it could be repaired easily enough.

Hays could see that the various teams had things more or less under control, so he just went around to thank them for their efforts, and left to drive back to the hospital.

* * *

"Hi, Maureen, you're looking a lot better. How's the ankle?" Hays said when he saw her sitting up in the chair beside her hospital bed.

"Sore, but the doctor said it will just take a few days, there's nothing broken. Look, Mick, I want to get out of here. Can we get back to Galway? Don't forget we still have a murderer and kidnapper to catch!"

"Yes, and we have to re-unite you with your car, and get you a new mobile phone amongst other things too."

"Shit, I forgot about the car. Look, can you get Sinéad to bring it back for me – I'm not up to driving with this ankle?" Lyons said, handing over the key from her jacket pocket.

"Sure. I'll give her a call. It's still over at the old petrol station. Look, Maureen, do you not think I should take you home? You need to rest. You've been up all night in that blasted bog after all."

"No, Superintendent, I don't. I'm fine, really. I appreciate your concern for a fellow officer, but I'm OK, really."

"You're incorrigible!" He leant over and kissed her gently.

* * *

When Lyons got back to the Garda station, she spoke to John O'Connor who looked after all the technology for the detectives.

"John, could you sort out a replacement phone for me when you get a second? I'm on the 3 network, and everything is backed up, so it should be easy enough. My number is in the system."

"Yes, sure, boss. That looks nasty. Are you OK?"

"Yes, thanks. I'll just have to use this crutch for a week or so. Damned nuisance. Can you round everyone up for me, John? I want to hold a briefing in ten minutes."

"Yes, sure."

Lyons' depleted team assembled in the open plan. They were glad to see that she was OK, and each one in turn asked how she was feeling, which, she had to admit to herself only, wasn't great.

On the way back to the city in the car Hays had tried to persuade Lyons to stay in hospital overnight, or at least go home and rest up after her ordeal, but she was having none of it.

"So, you want me to take to my bed with a vicious murderer out there somewhere, planning God knows what, and half the team away on jollies. You really don't know me that well at all, Mick, do you?" she responded rather gruffly to his suggestion.

"Oh, forgive me for caring, Maureen!"

They agreed to differ.

"Right, everyone. Firstly, thanks for your good wishes. I had a bad night, but I'm OK and we have a lot to do, so let's get on. Have we got recent photos of the suspect from his driving license?"

John O'Connor spoke up.

"We have, boss. It came across from the car hire company, but it's very poor. And there's nothing on our records because it's a forgery."

"Terrific! Did Sinéad get anything from the caravan or the car?"

Sally Fahy answered for Sinéad Loughran, who wasn't at the meeting.

"Sinéad got nothing from the mobile home. It was totally burnt out. But the car was a bit more productive. She has dabs and DNA from O'Malley, and Triona. She also said that she took some moulds from what looked like motorcycle tyres around the old shed."

"Mmm, well that ties in with what Mary Fallon recorded at the checkpoint outside Roundstone. So, that confirms what we thought. He's now going by the name of Derek Drummond, so let's get that out to everyone."

"Boss – what can you tell us from your encounter?" Sally Fahy said.

"Good question, Sally. Not a lot. He seems hell bent on revenge for the time I caught him robbing the bank. He wasn't very talkative," Lyons said.

"What about the girl on the beach?" Fahy went on.

"He just said that she was collateral damage. Apparently, he got frisky with her and she resisted, so he just bumped her off."

"A right little prince charming, isn't he?" Fahy said.

"You don't know the half of it – trust me. So – plans!" Lyons said. "Hotels, Airbnb's, guesthouses – we need to check them all to see if our Mr Drummond is resident in our midst. Get some help from uniform, but there won't be too many visitors at this time of year. I have a feeling I'll be the next person to encounter him, though I have absolutely no idea how that will come about!"

* * *

O'Malley was relieved to get through the checkpoint with such ease. But why not? After all, the Gardaí were looking for someone in a Fiat Punto – not a guy on a motorbike. And his new identity papers looked pretty good too – he had paid a lot for them. He had a small amount of cash left over from robberies he had committed before Lyons apprehended him on Eyre Square, but at the rate he was getting through it, it would need to be topped up soon.

He had done his research well. When he got clear of Connemara, and was approaching the outskirts of Galway city, he steered the bike onto a narrow dirt track that led him up behind Moycullen. He turned left again and soon came to a pair of chain-link gates that had once been padlocked, but were now hanging off their hinges. O'Malley rode the bike in through the gates, and dodged the many empty beer cans and broken vodka bottles strewn around. He pulled the Honda up at the lip of a deep quarry pit, filled with murky grey water and all sorts of miscellaneous detritus. He dismounted, switched the bike off, took the key out and gave it an almighty push; sending it descending in a steep arc till it hit the water. It disappeared with a massive splash and a small cloud of steam from the hot engine. He then took off his helmet and sent it in after the bike. It floated for a few moments, before turning over, filling with water and sinking to the murky depths. Pleased with his handiwork, he left the old quarry again and headed into town. It was time to put the next phase of his plan into action.

* * *

Mary Fallon was unhappy as she sat with Pascal Brosnan in the small Garda station on the edge of Roundstone.

"Damn it, Pascal, he shouldn't have slipped through my fingers that easily. I feel rotten."

"Don't be daft, girl. Sure, weren't we told to look out for a fella in a red Fiat Punto. We weren't to know he'd swapped it for two wheels. And you said the photo on his license was pretty useless. So it wasn't your fault. Don't beat yourself up over it," her colleague said.

"Still, I feel as if I've let the side down. And poor Inspector Lyons – that must have been awful for her. She probably thought she was going to die!"

"Nasty, all right. But I hear she's a very tough woman. She's been in a few scrapes over the years, and always seems to come out on top. She nearly got herself shot before during a robbery, and she was kidnapped another time too, but she always managed to get the boyos that were doing it. If I was O'Malley, I'd be worried."

* * *

O'Malley had checked himself into a hostel in the city under yet another assumed name. No one bothered to check his identification. The guy who was manning the desk rather unenthusiastically didn't seem to care, as long as the room was paid for in advance, and of course, in cash.

When he had deposited his stuff, O'Malley set out in search of a late-night chemist, and made a number of purchases, before returning to the hostel and using the fruits of his shopping to completely change his appearance. He used red hair dye to recolour his hair, cut it short, and shaved the three days of stubble off his face. Now looking like someone else altogether, he left the hostel again and set off in search of his next acquisition.

One of the many skills he had learned in prison was how to successfully steal a car in less than forty seconds. He had been given the privilege of working in the garage at the jail, where most of the work involved servicing the staff's cars. But part of the education he received from the other inmates was about car theft. Using very basic implements such as a wire coat hanger and a small screwdriver, O'Malley had learnt how to take certain makes of car in short order.

It didn't take him long to spot his quarry on the streets of Galway. A dark coloured 1998 Ford escort would do him nicely. It was parked in a quiet side street, and with no one around, and no sign of any CCTV anywhere, O'Malley put his lessons into practice. He was away in the car in under a minute.

He drove sedately to the outskirts of the city, pulling in at a large petrol station that was still open, despite the late hour. He put €30 worth of petrol into the stolen car and went inside as if to pay.

Once inside, he pulled his woolly hat down over his face, and took out the crowbar he had found in the back of the old Ford. He approached the counter with the bar raised and shouted at the poor unfortunate behind the till.

"Don't press the alarm, just give me the cash and I won't hurt you. Now!!!"

The bewildered cashier was scared stiff. He quickly opened the till and handed out its contents to O'Malley who stuffed the money into his jacket pocket.

"Give me five minutes before you call the cops. No messing, or I'll come back for you. Got it?"

The cashier nodded, seeing the wildness in O'Malley's eyes. He had no doubt that the man meant it.

When O'Malley got clear of the area he pulled over to the side of the road and counted his haul. He had collected just over €1,400 from the petrol station in used notes.

"Excellent. That will do me nicely," he said, smiling to himself.

Knowing that the car's registration would have been recorded on camera at the filling station, he needed to get rid of it as soon as possible. He drove back out to the quarry where he had disposed of the motorbike, and did the same with the car. The pit must have been very deep, because as soon as the car hit the water, it upended with the bonnet disappearing, and the rest of it sliding down into the dirty water.

O'Malley turned on his heels, and like the stolen car, disappeared into the night.

Chapter Twenty-Four

"Are you sure you're OK to go to work, love?" Hays said to Lyons the following morning at breakfast.

Lyons had strapped her ankle up with a strong elastic bandage, and was able to put some weight on it now, but she still had to be careful. She could get around without the aid of a crutch, but progress was slower than normal, and quite painful. However, she wasn't about to admit that to Hays.

"Yes thanks, I'm fine. Just a bit tender, but it's much better. I'll be grand."

"Are you OK to drive? I have to go to Athlone for a meeting, and I'll probably have to stay over if it goes on late. I'm sure you could get Sally to stay with you, if you like."

"Look, Mick, I'm fine. Don't fuss. What's the scene in Athlone anyway?"

"The Commissioner wants us to look at merging the west and north-west crime regions. It's just a paper exercise for now, but if I know anything, it will turn into something more before long. I'm not keen to be honest, and Finbarr is hopping mad. He says he'll retire if that happens."

"I'm sure you'll be able to scupper it; aren't you?" Lyons said.

"Almost certainly, but not for a while yet. We'll have to waste a year or so with endless consultants and spend a small fortune before it will be deemed impractical. You know how these things go."

"Hmph. Not much to do with thief taking, is it?"

"You can say that again. Anyway, I must be off. Are you sure you're OK? Will I get a car out to take you into Mill Street?"

"No, don't do that. Remember, I'm supposed to be invincible. I don't want my reputation ruined!"

"Very well. I'll call you later." He took her in his arms and gave her an affectionate kiss and a long hug before departing.

* * *

Lyons got to work thirty minutes later. Driving had been more awkward and painful than she had hoped, but she was damned if she was going to give in to it. Before she got out of the car in the station car park, she swallowed two paracetamol.

She struggled up the stairs and made it to her office, glad for the chance to sit down while the pills were taking effect. Sally Fahy appeared at the door.

"Hi, Sally. What's new? Anything in overnight?" Lyons said.

"No, 'fraid not, boss. There was a robbery out at that gas station on the Headford road, but uniform are dealing with it. That's about it."

"Not again! How much was taken this time?" Lyons said.

"Well, the night man said just over three thousand euro, but it seems like a lot to me."

"Yeah, me too. Any CCTV?"

"Yes, but according to Sergeant O'Toole, it's useless. Do you think we should go out and talk to the guy who was on the till? Apparently, he's back on at eleven o'clock," Fahy said.

"Probably. Let's see what the day brings. You couldn't do me a big favour, Sally?"

"Sure, what do you need?"

"Coffee, and it's urgent!"

Fahy smiled and said, "Right. I'll pop across the road and get a nice strong Americano. Would you like anything with it? A muffin maybe?"

"No thanks. Just had breakfast. Here, get yourself one too." She handed Fahy a €10 note.

* * *

As Lyons and Fahy were finishing their coffee, John O'Connor came into the office holding up a DVD.

"CCTV from the petrol station. You said you wanted to see it when it came in, boss."

"Oh, yes, thanks John. Give it here," Lyons said, holding out her hand.

She put the DVD into the drive on her computer and the two detectives watched as it whirred into action. Then, a rather snowy image appeared on the PC's screen.

"I've cut out everything except the bit where our hero arrives," O'Connor said.

The two women watched the video in silence. When the bandit had come running out of the shop attached to the petrol station, and was getting back into the stolen Ford, Lyons suddenly exclaimed, "Stop it. Just there. Look at his shoes. Can you zoom in on them Sally?"

Fahy prodded a few keys on the PC and moved the mouse around the desk until she had an enlarged image of the thief's feet in the centre of the screen.

"It's him! I saw those trainers just before he knocked me out. They're quite distinctive with that blue and red stripe. That's O'Malley!"

"Are you sure, boss? It's very hard to see."

"No, I'm sure. When he grabbed me from behind out at Mannin, I was determined to inflict some pain on him, so I looked down at his feet before stamping hard on his left shoe – that's definitely the same trainer," Lyons said.

"Wow. Can you make out the registration number of the car?" Fahy said.

"No, but get John to see if he can enhance the picture a bit. That's why they have those cameras there in any case – to capture reg. numbers of people who drive off without paying."

Fahy stopped the video and removed the disc, taking it to John O'Connor.

"John, can you see if you can get a reg. number from this tape? And if you can, find out anything you can about the car," Fahy said.

* * *

An hour later, Lyons was sitting in her office. The tablets were beginning to wear off, and she was feeling quite sorry for herself, more from the lack of progress than anything else.

John O'Connor came back into the office.

"I got the number of that car at the petrol station. It was stolen in the city last night. I spoke to the owner – seems straight forward enough. He was having a meal in town and when he came out to go home, his car was gone. He reported it at around 11:15, and he's not known to us, so it seems OK."

"Right. Well, put out an all-points bulletin for the car anyway. I doubt if O'Malley has gone sight-seeing in it to be honest, but it's worth a try."

"Right, boss. Are you OK?"

"Sort of, John. I'd be fine if we could actually catch this bugger!"

* * *

The day wore on slowly, with little progress in any direction. Lyons' ankle was sore as hell. Every time she got up from her desk, she got a nasty twinge of pain which made her humour even more grave.

There were no sightings of either the stolen car or O'Malley, even though the Gardaí had more or less swamped the area and circulated pictures of him all across town. By five o'clock Lyons was feeling grim, and decided to call it a day.

"I'm going home, Sally. I've had enough for today. Let's hope for better luck tomorrow. If anything breaks, give me a call. John got me a new mobile, but it's the same number."

"OK, boss. See you tomorrow."

Chapter Twenty-Five

Lyons got home before six o'clock. She was feeling quite miserable, and definitely not up to cooking. When she had changed out of her work clothes into a comfy pair of jeans and a jumper, she took a frozen lasagne out of the freezer and popped it in the microwave. She assembled a plate of salad with lettuce, tomatoes, scallions, olives, and a few slices of fresh orange while the lasagne was heating up.

When the oven pinged, she took a bottle of red wine that was already open and poured a generous measure. She ate the meal with little enthusiasm, leaving a quarter of it unfinished on the kitchen table, and went into the lounge. She turned on the telly, but paid no attention to whatever nonsense was showing. Her mind wandered back to recent events, as she tried to figure out how she might be able to apprehend O'Malley before he did any further damage.

Her new mobile phone started chirping beside her on the sofa. It was an unfamiliar ringtone, and for a few seconds she didn't realise what it was. Then she picked it up, and answered it.

"Lyons."

"Hi. It's me. How's things?" Hays said.

"Oh, hi Mick. Grand, I'm fine really. Just had something to eat, and sitting here watching some dreadful crap on TV. What about you?"

"Much as predicted. The younger guys are all excited, but the rest of the old timers recognize this for what it is, so we're pretty bored to be honest. But I'm not going to make it back tonight, I'm afraid. Will you be OK?"

"Yeah, sure. Don't worry about me. Just look after yourself. I'll see you tomorrow – but, Mick?"

"Yes?"

"That doesn't mean I'm not missing you," she said.

"Me too, love. Are you sure you wouldn't like someone to stay with you? I'm sure Sally would be happy to come out to you. The two of you might even have some fun!"

"Nah, I'm OK – really. I'm pretty knackered to be honest. I'll go off to bed soon and let's hope I sleep through."

"OK, then. I'll let you get on. Love you."

"You too. Goodnight."

Lyons stayed watching TV for a bit longer, but she was drifting off to sleep in front of it, so she decided to give in to it and head upstairs. She was glad to be back in her own comfortable bed, even if the other half of it was unoccupied. She really was very tired, and almost as soon as her head hit the pillow, she fell into a deep sleep.

* * *

Lyons woke with a start. The green glow of the alarm clock on the night stand indicated 2:40. At first, she wondered what had woken her, but then she heard it. It

161

wasn't loud, but there was definitely some muffled noise coming from downstairs. Luckily, Lyons had rehearsed exactly what she would do in these circumstances several times in her own mind, so she set to work very quietly.

A few minutes later, there was a tiny creek on the landing outside her bedroom door. The door opened silently, and a dark figure entered.

"Gotcha, you bitch," O'Malley said as he lunged at the prone form in the bed, and drove the long blade of the kitchen knife into it three times with tremendous force.

Lyons switched on the bedside light that she had taken across to the dressing table.

"Good morning, Mr O'Malley," she said.

O'Malley spun round, not quite knowing what the hell was happening. He assumed, after all, that he had killed her.

Lyons was sitting in the bedroom chair in her dressing gown. She had her Sig Sauer pistol aimed squarely at the intruder.

O'Malley was quick. He grabbed the bolster that he had stabbed from the bed, and threw it at Lyons, following up by coming in behind it, the knife held out in front of him. Feathers flew everywhere, and for a moment, Lyons vision was blurred. She fired the gun.

The noise was deafening in the small room, and the blowback from the gun sent the feathers from the pillows into a frenzy. Lyons couldn't see exactly where she had hit the target, but she knew from his reaction that her aim had not been far off.

O'Malley screamed, dropped the knife, and put his right hand to his left bicep which was pouring blood through the ragged edges of a large hole in his jacket.

"Fuck you!" he screamed, and ran from the room, down the stairs and out through the open front door.

* * *

Hays was uneasy about leaving Maureen Lyons alone at home after the ordeal she had been through. His meeting had gone on until nearly midnight, punctuated by a couple of hours when the delegates stopped for a sumptuous meal. But when they finally brought matters to a close, Hays decided he would travel home to Galway. As he had been drinking, he arranged for a uniformed driver from the local station to do the driving, and the two set off at a brisk pace, making good time with little traffic to impede their progress.

With an ironic sense of timing, Hays' Audi A6 pulled up outside his house in Salthill just seconds after O'Malley had made his escape. As the car came to a halt, Hays noticed that his front door was open, and the light was on in the bedroom he shared with Lyons at the front of the house.

Fearing something dreadful, he leapt from the car and ran into the house shouting, "Maureen, Maureen. Where are you? Are you OK?"

"Up here, in the bedroom," she responded loudly, recognising her partner's voice.

Hays took the stairs two at a time and burst into their bedroom to see Lyons still sitting in the chair cradling her pistol in her hand. The veritable cloud of feathers and dust that had been stirred up had settled, with several feathers from the burst pillow landing in Lyons' dark brown hair.

"Christ, are you hurt, love?" Hays demanded as he went across the room and embraced her.

"You should see the other fellow!" she said, speaking into the shoulder of his jacket as he continued to embrace her.

Hays stood back, and said, "What the hell happened?"

"No time for that now, Mick. I had a nocturnal visitor. But as you can see he's wounded, so we need to get the troops out to round him up. Can you get on the blower?"

Hays didn't need any further prompting. He called Mill Street on his mobile, and spoke in urgent terms to the night sergeant.

"I want the area around here swamped with every man you can get out, Dermot. And quickly. Then I want you to get onto Joe Mason and get him down here with his dog as fast as you can. There's a wounded suspect on the run, and he's bleeding from a gunshot wound, so Joe should be able to track him if he gets here soon."

"Right, sir. I'm on it. Do we need the Armed Response Unit too?"

"No, not yet anyway. Our client is only armed with a knife, and he's probably dumped that by now anyway. I'll leave you to it, Sergeant."

Within minutes three squad cars arrived at Hays' and Lyons' house in Salthill with their blue lights flashing. Hays rattled out instructions in short order, and the uniformed men set off in various directions, attempting to pick up the trail of blood spots left on the footpath by the fleeing O'Malley.

A few minutes later, Mason's little white van arrived, and Joe wasted no time in getting Brutus out from his cage in the back. The dog was all business-like, eagerly looking to his handler for instructions.

By this time Lyons had appeared, still in her dressing gown and slippers, at the front door.

"Hi, Joe; Brutus. I think I shot him in the left arm. He's obviously bleeding quite badly. Can you two get after the trail?"

"Right. C'mon fella, let's go." Joe pointed Brutus at the spots of blood on the footpath. The dog needed no second invitation and the pair of them set off at a brisk trot with Brutus' nose close to the ground.

* * *

"Damn that bitch!" O'Malley said as he ran back along the seafront away from Lyons' house. His arm was hurting like hell, and it was bleeding profusely, to the extent that he was already beginning to feel light-headed.

He cut up an alleyway that was lined with green and black wheelie bins. The lane was very poorly lit, and when he got a good distance from the lights along the promenade, he slouched down between two bins to collect his thoughts and see if he could render himself some basic first aid.

He managed to wriggle out of his jacket, and using his teeth and his one remaining working arm, he ripped the right-hand sleeve out of his shirt. The pain was excruciating as he tied the torn shirt sleeve around the top of his left arm and pulled it tight, again using his teeth to create a makeshift tourniquet in an effort to stop the bleeding. It worked, in a sort of a way. The bleeding slowed. O'Malley sat there on the ground catching his breath, and waiting until he had recovered a little from the shock. After a few minutes, he managed to get upright, and leaving his jacket behind, set off, stumbling over his own feet, down the lane. He knew he needed to get clear of the area, but his original plan, which was to take Lyons' car after he had disposed of her, was obviously out of the question now.

The alley he was in ran along behind a row of houses, and several of them had garages that opened onto it. O'Malley tried each of them, and after a few attempts, he found one that wasn't locked. He struggled with the door using his good arm, and managed to prise it open enough for him to get in. The garage was more or less empty, but at the back there was another door which led to the garden of the house to which it belonged. He tried the handle, and to his relief it opened. Once in the garden, O'Malley found a garden shed, and was surprised to find that it too was not fully secured. He slid the bolt to the side, opened the door, entered the shed and pulled the door closed behind him. At last he was safe, for now at least.

* * *

Hays and Lyons were now seated at the kitchen table. Hays had made strong coffee for them both, and he had removed the white feathers from Lyons' hair.

"So, tell me what happened, love?"

Lyons related her story about how she was awoken some time after 2 a.m. by a noise downstairs. Given recent events, she calculated that it could easily have been O'Malley who had clearly broken in, and she went about preparing the bedroom. She placed the bolster down inside the duvet so that it looked as if the bed was occupied, and she took her pistol from its safe behind the dressing table and sat down to wait for him.

"Did you intend to shoot him in the arm?" Hays said.

166

"I don't know. To be honest, Mick, I think if I had been able to see properly, I could easily have shot him in the head. I was very pissed off with him. I still am. Perhaps it worked out well in the end. A dead body would have been hard to explain to Plunkett, whereas a wounding just looks like reasonable force, in self-defence. Anyway, how come you came back?"

"I just had this uneasy feeling about you. I wasn't happy with you being here on your own after what happened. Just as well too, by the look of things. Thank God you're all right."

"Ah, I'm a tough old bird, Mick. It'll take more than the likes of him to put me away. But I'm glad I'm a light sleeper."

"Hmmm, well we'll talk about this later. Finish your coffee and let's see how the lads are getting on. O'Malley can't have got far."

* * *

Brutus successfully tracked the spots of blood on the paths, and led Joe to the laneway where O'Malley had stopped to patch himself up. Brutus sniffed around for quite a while at this location, as if he was re-programming his senses to continue the search, relying now on the scent from the person himself.

The dog moved off again, going more slowly this time, and stopped again when they reached the garage door. He looked up at Mason, as if to ask his handler to open it. Joe levered the door open, and Brutus went in. At this stage, Joe knew that Brutus would probably do better on his own, so he bent down and released the dog's lead, leaving

Brutus free to go wherever he wanted, and at his own pace.

Brutus squeezed out through the back door of the garage into the garden, and made straight for the small wooden shed. He started scratching at the door with his front paws.

Inside the shed, O'Malley, who was now feeling very weak and dizzy, just managed to croak, "Fuck off!" in a hoarse whisper.

Joe opened the shed door, and the dog started barking wildly and baring his impressive array of very sharp teeth at O'Malley.

O'Malley reached out and found a garden fork, and tried to prod Brutus in the face, but the dog dodged the weapon easily. But now feeling threatened, Brutus leapt forward and sank his teeth into the right arm of his attacker, and held it firmly. Brutus was making terrifying growling noises as he held his prey between his jaws.

"Jesus, get him off. He's biting me. Get the fucking thing off me!" O'Malley shrieked.

Joe Mason didn't hurry to oblige. He made sure that O'Malley was thoroughly disabled, before taking handcuffs from his belt and instructing O'Malley to turn over on his stomach with his hands behind his back. He then called Brutus off, and the dog obeyed by letting go of O'Malley's arm. Brutus retreated to just outside the shed and lay down on the grass keeping a good watch on his handler and the suspect in case trouble broke out again.

Joe radioed to his colleagues, and within a few minutes a white Garda van drove up the lane to collect its somewhat damaged cargo.

Chapter Twenty-Six

Lyons was still hobbling a little on her sprained ankle as she went to work the following day. They had finally got to sleep soon after 5 a.m., having gone into the spare room, their own bedroom being cordoned off as a crime scene. In any case, it was in disarray with feathers everywhere and bloodstains on the carpet.

Sinéad Loughran was despatched, along with two of her team, to collect forensic evidence from the house in Salthill. O'Malley had dropped the knife he was intending to use to stab Lyons, and they would need to collect fingerprints from it.

The garage and the shed at the back of the house where O'Malley had been captured was also of interest to the forensic team.

O'Malley had been taken in the Garda van to the Regional Hospital where the night crew had dressed his wounded arm and given him an anti-tetanus injection. His injuries were deemed to be non-life threatening, and he was discharged back into the custody of the Gardaí shortly before breakfast.

When Lyons was settled behind her desk, Sally Fahy came into her office.

"Jesus, boss, you've been through the wars. Are you OK?"

"Hi, Sally. Yes, I'm fine thanks. Where's O'Malley?"

"He's downstairs. Are you going to interview him, or would you like someone else to do it?"

"No, it's OK. I'll do it, but I need to see Chief Superintendent Plunkett first. He's been asking for me."

"Oh, right. Good luck with that!"

"Ah, it'll be fine. At least he's unlikely to try and stab me!"

Lyons ascended the stairs to Chief Superintendent Finbarr Plunkett's plush office on the third floor, still wincing a little from her injury. She knocked on the polished mahogany door, and waited to be invited in.

"Ah, Maureen, come in, come in. Take a seat. Can I get you a coffee?" Plunkett said.

"No thanks, sir. I've just had one downstairs."

"Oh, OK. Well now, how are you feeling?"

"I'm OK, sir. Still a bit sore from that episode in the bog, and last night was a bit crazy, but I'm OK."

"Good woman. That's the spirit. I was just talking to Superintendent Hays about the case. What is it that you're intending to charge this – what's his name – O'Malley with?"

"It's going to be a long rap sheet, sir. There's the murder of the girl out at Ballyconneely to begin with. Then there's the kidnapping of Triona Fox. After that, he kidnapped me, and we have the robbery at the petrol

170

station and the car theft to lay at his door too. And to top it all off we have the attempted murder of a serving officer, sir."

"Hmm, I see what you mean. And how are we with evidence for this catalogue of crimes?" Plunkett said.

"It will take a good deal more work to get our ducks in a row, sir. We have forensics that link him directly to the murder of Sheena Finnegan, and he rather foolishly sent me a lock of Triona's hair in the post. But the robberies are more difficult, and to be honest, I haven't begun to put the evidence of last night's little caper together. But that won't be a problem. He dropped his weapon near the scene, and there's plenty of blood evidence too."

"That's what I wanted to talk to you about. As you know, we have to be very careful about the use of our resources these days. And after all, if you get him on the murder of the girl, he'll get life anyway, so do you think it's worthwhile pursuing all the other stuff with the amount of work it will involve for us?"

"Sorry, sir. Are you suggesting we overlook several of these crimes? And anyway, isn't there a possibility that the judge could apply the sentences consecutively? That's allowed these days, and that would take him off the streets for the rest of his natural life."

"Well, of course, Maureen it's up to you. But there's something else."

"Yes, sir, and what's that?"

"Last night. I understand he broke into your house and was planning to stab you, and that you repelled him by shooting him in the arm. Is that how it went?"

"Well, yes, sir. That's a brief description. Why?" Lyons said.

"Well, it's just that it's not going to look too good in the papers. And I understand O'Malley was attacked by Joe Mason's dog too during the arrest. It's not good that a serious criminal was able to get into the house of two senior officers and nearly kill one of them. And it will bring the whole business of you and Hays living together into focus too. It could be very awkward."

Lyons was horrified. She couldn't believe what Plunkett was saying, but somehow managed not to erupt into a rage. Her neck and face did get very red though. Plunkett saw the signs and had no intention of being 'Maureened'.

"Tell you what," he said hurriedly, "why don't you give it some thought? Talk it over with Mick and let me know what you decide. I know you'll make the right decision in the best interest of us all."

Plunkett then looked down at the surface of his desk and started to shuffle his papers about. This was his way of signalling that the meeting was over, and Lyons got the message.

"Very well, sir. Will that be all?"

"Yes, thanks, oh and Maureen – well done. I'm glad you caught him, and didn't come to any real harm."

* * *

When Lyons got back downstairs, she was furious. She stomped back into her office, and Sally Fahy came in after her.

"Are you OK, boss?"

"No, Sally, I'm bloody well not! I swear, I'll swing for that man one of these days. He only wants me to drop half the charges we have against O'Malley! The cheek. It wasn't

172

him that nearly got carved open or spent the night in a bloody bog hole!"

"Oh shit. Listen, can I get you a coffee?" Fahy said, desperate to try and placate her boss in some small way.

"No, I'm fine thanks, Sally. Sorry for sounding off. Do you know if Mick is around?"

"I'll find out. Do you want to see him if he is?"

"Yes, I bloody do!"

"OK. I'll be right back."

Lyons tried to calm down before she got speaking to Mick Hays. Although they were life partners, he was still her senior officer, and she didn't want to tear into him too severely. She was working out a strategy when her phone rang.

"Hi," Hays said, "you were looking for me."

"Mick, yeah. We need to talk. Have you a few minutes?"

"Sure. What about Darcy's?" Hays said.

"Great. See you in a few minutes. Thanks."

They found a nice quiet spot in the little coffee bar close to the Garda station.

"What's up?" Hays asked when they had been served two mugs of filter coffee.

Lyons relayed the conversation that she had had with Finbarr Plunkett not an hour previously, and made it abundantly clear that she was very unhappy at his suggestion.

"I can see where you're coming from, Maureen. I mean we go to extreme lengths to bring these scumbags to book, and then we get half of it thrown in our faces. Talk about demotivational! And as usual, you have gone well above and beyond. It's definitely not fair. Would you like me to have a word?"

"Actually, I was going to suggest a slightly different approach, Mick. Honestly – what do you think would be the appropriate charges to bring against O'Malley, given Plunkett's misgivings about last night?" Lyons said.

"Hmm, that's a tricky one. Definitely the murder of Sheena Finnegan. Definitely the kidnap of the girl. Then, if we could bundle up the various attempts he made on you into something that nobody will easily understand – only if you're OK with it – that might keep everyone happy. What do you think?"

"I knew you'd have some good ideas. That sounds just about right to me. Something like perverting the course of justice, obstructing the Gardaí – that sort of thing?"

"Yeah. I'd probably throw in assaulting a police officer too just for good measure, and maybe a few other titbits. Or maybe assaulting a pillow and a mattress!" he said smiling.

"Fuck off, Hays! But you're right, that sounds like a plan. Nice one, Superintendent!"

Chapter Twenty-Seven

Edward Mulvaney was seated beside Eoin O'Malley in the interview room when Lyons and her new protégé entered. Mulvaney was a young duty solicitor, learning his trade. Lyons had encountered him before, and while he was young and almost cherub like in appearance, he could be tricky enough.

Lyons had briefed Dermot Heffernan before starting the interview, instructing him to say nothing unless he was specifically addressed, but to watch for Lyons' signal for him to take over questioning of the suspect, if required.

"Before we begin," Mulvaney said, trying to sound authoritative, "my client would like to express his profound regret at the drowning of the girl at the beach in Ballyconneely. It was a pure accident, of course. He had no idea that the tide would submerge the car like that, and when it happened, he just panicked and fled the scene. He's very sorry, and wished he had behaved differently."

"So do we all, Mr Mulvaney, so do we all. But I'm afraid your client has misinformed you, Mr Mulvaney," Lyons said.

"I hardly think so, Inspector. What do you mean?"

"Sheena Finnegan – the girl that died out at Ballyconneely – didn't drown. She was attacked, hit so hard that one of her front teeth was knocked out, and then she was strangled with your client's bare hands. Before he fled, that is."

Mulvaney shot an angry glance at O'Malley, but managed to retain his composure.

"And I presume you have evidence to back up this accusation, Inspector," Mulvaney said.

"Certainly, we have. Sufficient to charge your client with murder which I will be doing shortly. Now let's get on. Tell me about the second girl that you abducted, Mr O'Malley."

Again, Mulvaney intervened.

"My client abducted no one, Inspector. The girl you are referring to took a lift with my client, and went back to his temporary dwelling willingly, and chose to remain there overnight."

"Really. And did she decide to bind her hands and feet with duct tape and chain herself up as well?"

Mulvaney remained silent, but O'Malley said, "No comment."

"I'm not sure if you are aware of the penalties that go with child abduction, Mr O'Malley, but you're looking at a minimum of fifteen years and I'll be suggesting that your various sentences run consecutively, so it could be a long time you see daylight again, if ever."

Lyons waited for this to sink in, when Mulvaney spoke up again.

"What exactly is it that you want from my client, Inspector? Oh, and by the way, we intend to pursue the injury that my client received at your home when you shot him in the arm, totally unprovoked," he asked.

"I would suggest that you don't go there, Mr Mulvaney. Your client broke into my home and was intent on stabbing me to death, as witnessed by the damage he did to my bed. When he came at me with a knife having failed to stab me when he thought I was asleep, I fired at him in self-defence, making sure not to endanger his life."

Mulvaney grunted, but said nothing.

Lyons tapped Heffernan on the ankle under the table.

"We would like your client to co-operate. If he was prepared to plead guilty to murder, kidnapping, robbery and the attempted murder of a serving member of the Garda Síochána, breaking and entering and car theft, we would be happy to tell the court of his co-operation when the matter comes before them," Heffernan said.

Lyons was a bit surprised that he had disclosed all the information that they had on O'Malley, but what harm? It would all come out during the interview in any case.

Mulvaney looked at O'Malley, who stared back showing no emotion.

"I would like some time to confer with my client, Inspector," Mulvaney said.

"Certainly, but not yet. I want to know where your client procured a false driving license and passport. We can't have these things circulating unchecked, it would create mayhem. We also want to know where he got the motorbike – I presume it was stolen – and where it is now, as well as the Ford that he lifted in Galway. And, of course, we want the €3,000 that he stole from the petrol station back as well. So that will give you something to talk about for a few minutes – shall we say half an hour?"

Lyons and Heffernan left the interview room and returned to the open plan where Sally Fahy was waiting anxiously to know how things were going.

"I'm not sure, to be honest, Sally. I expect Mulvaney will come up with some bullshit to try and get the little weasel off, or at least a significantly reduced sentence. Let's see. Anything happening here?"

"Superintendent Hays was looking for you, but he said it's not urgent if you're busy. He'll call you later," Fahy said.

"Oh, and Sinéad was on. They have confirmed that the skin flakes taken from Sheena's earring are a match for O'Malley's DNA, as is the hair we found stuck to the padded envelope."

"Excellent. C'mon, Dermot, let's get a coffee and then we'll get back to it," Lyons said.

* * *

When the interview resumed, Lyons asked Mulvaney if he would like to tell them to which crimes O'Malley was prepared to plead guilty.

"My client believes that the death of the girl in the car on the beach was an unfortunate accident, but an accident nevertheless. He is prepared to admit to the theft of money from the petrol station, but insists that he only got €1,400, not €3,000. And he will admit to assaulting a member of the Gardaí Síochána – namely your good self."

Lyons stared incredulously at the solicitor.

"Is that it? What about kidnap, vehicle theft, breaking and entering and all the other stuff we have on him?"

Mulvaney said nothing.

"Firstly, regarding Sheena Finnegan who was murdered in the car at Ballyconneely. We now know that one of her earrings was ripped from her ear lobe post-mortem, and that it was sent to me by your client in a padded envelope. So, we know that she was dead when the earring was removed, and together with the fact that she didn't drown, but was strangled, proves conclusively that your client is the killer. So, we'll be sticking with murder on that one. Now what else is he prepared to confess to?"

Mulvaney looked at his client, but O'Malley didn't respond.

"Right, Dermot, charge Mr O'Malley here with everything we've got on him so far. Everything. We should be able to get him into court later, and by the way, Mr Mulvaney, we will of course be opposing bail."

* * *

Back in her office, Lyons called Sally Fahy in to speak to her.

"You know, Sally, there's something bothering me. A kind of stone in my shoe, if you like," Lyons said.

"What's that, boss?"

"That petrol station that O'Malley turned over. You know we were surprised at the amount of money that they reported stolen? O'Malley said he only got €1,400. Why don't we go out and have a chat to whoever is on duty there? I smell a rat."

The two detectives drove out to the petrol station on the Headford Road that O'Malley had robbed. The introduced himself to the man behind the cash desk, who looked as if he might have originally come from India.

"May I have your name, please?" Fahy asked.

"Vihaan Patel. I'm from Kerala in India," the man said.

"Thanks, Vihaan. How long have you been working here?" Lyons asked.

"I'm here nearly four years now. I work seven to four on days, and four to midnight when I'm doing nights."

"And can I ask how many robberies there have been here at the station since you started working here?" Fahy said.

"Oh, goodness, too many for me. Must be six or seven at least," Patel said.

"Really? And have you been on duty when these robberies have happened, Vihaan?" Fahy said.

"Sometimes, yes."

"And how much is taken when these robberies happen?" Lyons said.

At this, the man became a little coy. He looked down at his feet, and was slow to answer.

"It varies. Sometimes a lot, sometimes a little. Depends," he said, still not looking at either Lyons or Fahy.

"But you always report the same amount, Vihaan. It's always €3,000, isn't it?" Lyons said.

"Boss tells me always to say three thousand. Something to do with insurance he says."

"Really! But that's not very truthful, Vihaan. Are you OK with that?" Fahy said.

"No, not really. But I need the work, and he says the insurance pays up to that amount, so it's no harm."

"Where can we find your boss, Vihaan?" Lyons said.

"Hold on. I have a card here, and I can give you his phone number too," Patel said, now keen to assist the Gardaí, as if to make amends for his wrongdoing.

"Thanks."

Lyons turned to Fahy and said, "Why don't you take Dermot out to have a chat with this geezer when we get back to the station. It will be good for Heffernan to have an easy one to get him settled in. Book the guy and then pass it on to the fraud squad."

Chapter Twenty-Eight

O'Malley was brought before the court where it took quite some time to read out the long list of charges against the man. Hays had spoken to Lyons before they went to the courthouse, and they had agreed to leave out any reference to O'Malley's attack on her, or the episode where he broke into their house and tried to kill her. They had enough on O'Malley to get him put away for a very long time indeed, without the potential embarrassment of the events at their home being raked over by the press.

"It will keep Plunkett happy in any case, and I'd rather not have the journos camped outside for two days," Hays said.

"Yeah, I guess. Best not to let everyone know I keep a gun there too. But it's all in order. I have the paperwork."

"I'm sure you have! I'll just have to be careful coming home from the pub late at night, knowing that you're armed to the teeth!"

"Oh, don't worry, Mick, if I'm going to shoot you it won't be in the arm! Go on – I'll see you later."

The judge agreed to hold O'Malley on remand, given that he was deemed to be a flight risk. It would take the Gardaí some time to prepare the book of evidence. He was remanded to appear again in a fortnight's time by video link from Castlerea, the nearest remand centre for male prisoners.

It was an hour and a half's drive from Galway to the remand centre. O'Malley was handcuffed to a uniformed Garda who took him out the side door of the courthouse to the waiting Transit van.

O'Malley had the handcuffs removed as he was placed in the back of the van where there was a cage not unlike the one in which Brutus spent much of his time, if a bit bigger.

It was late in the afternoon when the van set off, and the rain was pelting down, making driving conditions poor. Just north of Cloonfad, at a small four-way crossroads, a tractor drove out unexpectedly in front of the Garda van. The driver of the van swerved violently to avoid a collision, but the van mounted the ditch on the left-hand side, rose up in the air, and landed on its roof in a shower of sparks and smoke. The driver and the other Garda in the front seat survived. They were quite badly injured, with a lot of bruising, but they staggered from the wreck to find the tractor driver who by that time had vanished into the countryside.

O'Malley didn't fare as well. Although there was a seat belt provided for him in the back of the van, he hadn't fastened it, and when the crash came, he was hurled violently against the cage and his neck snapped. He was later pronounced dead by the ambulance crew that attended the scene of the accident.

*　*　*

When the news of the accident got back to Galway, there was a bit of an anti-climax amongst the team. In one way they were happy that the matter had been brought to an end, but they would have preferred to have their day in court, if for no other reason than to send a message to the criminal fraternity that crime doesn't pay.

A few days later, Lyons was sitting at her desk when her phone rang.

"Hi, it's me. Got a minute?" Hays said.

"Sure. Shall I pop up?"

"Yes, would you? I have the coffee brewing."

"Great. See you in a sec."

Lyons noticed that she was able to climb the stairs to Hays' office on the third floor of the Garda station with complete ease, now that her ankle had fully healed. She went into his office without knocking, and was surprised to see Chief Superintendent Finbarr Plunkett seated in front of Hays' desk.

"Oh, sorry, sir," Lyons said, swiftly abandoning her plan to give Hays a big hug and a kiss.

"Come in, Maureen. How's the foot?" Plunkett said.

"Fine, thanks, sir."

"Well, come in and sit down. I have some news for you. For you both really," Plunkett said.

When Lyons was seated, wondering what on earth could be coming at her, Plunkett went on. "I've been doing a bit of work behind the scenes for you. I wasn't happy that your home was violated by that low-life, O'Malley, even though he got his just deserts in the end. I had a word up above, and I've managed to get a bit of compensation for the injuries that you suffered in the bog, and at home. It's not a fortune, but it will buy you a new set of pillows in any case," Plunkett said.

"Finbarr has a cheque here for you for €10,000, Maureen," said Hays, holding up the piece of paper with the Garda logo embossed on its face.

"Wow. Thank you very much, sir. That's very generous. Thanks a lot."

"You deserve it, girl. Oh, and that other matter at the petrol station was spot on too. Yer man has been at it for a good few years, and the insurance company are prosecuting him. We have someone looking into the planning activity out in Clifden as well. All in all, a pretty good result, wouldn't you say?"

"I'd forgotten about the planning thing with all the fuss. But, yes. I'd say Jeremiah Breslin might be feeling a bit uncomfortable one of these days," Lyons said.

"He most certainly will! Well, that's me done. Thanks for all your good work, Maureen, and don't spend it all at once," Plunkett said, standing up and shaking hands with them both, before leaving the office.

Lyons finally got to hug her partner and plant that kiss on his very welcoming lips.

"What are we going to do with all that money, Maureen?"

"Oh no you don't. That's mine – all mine, Hays. Hands off!" she said, and kissed him again.

* * *

Lyons had decided, after the anti-climax of the road accident that had claimed the life of the killer, that she would take a few days off work.

"What will you do with your time off?" Hays said at breakfast.

"I might drive out to Athenry to see Sheila. She's been on the phone dead worried. I need to show her I'm still in one piece!"

"Ah, that sounds nice. Be sure to remember me to her. And if you want to stay out there tonight, that's fine too. Just let me know."

"Ah, no, you're grand. I'd rather be back here in my own bed with you, to be honest. Unless of course we go out on the razz," she said, smiling.

Hays left for work, and when he was well clear of the house, Lyons put her plan into action.

She phoned the brokerage in Galway and made an appointment to see the owner whom she had met once or twice with Hays at the yacht club.

An hour later, she was sitting in the man's office, surrounded by large photographs of yachts under full sail, and smiling families in the bright blue Mediterranean sunshine.

"So, Maureen, you want to arrange a surprise for Mick then? Is it that Beneteau 28?" he asked.

"Yeah – he's been talking about it all summer. He's really set on it. Assuming you were able to take the Folkboat in part exchange, what would we be talking about?"

"Well, I have that six-year-old one on the books at the moment. The owner sadly passed away, and the wife is keen to dispose of the boat. It's not doing it any good not being used. Of course, we want to be fair to her, but for a quick sale, I'd say she'd settle for quite a modest price."

"So, what are we talking about then?" Lyons said.

"Let me make a phone call. Could you drop back in the afternoon? I'll have the figures worked out by then. I need to do a proper appraisal on Mick's boat. I know he keeps it in good condition, but I'd like to look it over briefly."

"OK. But if by any chance you bump into him – not a word, OK? This is a surprise."

When Lyons called back in the afternoon, the broker had done all the sums and presented her with the result. It would consume a goodly portion of her windfall, but she reckoned it was worth it. She was so very grateful for the support and inspiration that Hays always provided for her, and just at this moment, she was glad to be alive as well. After a brief negotiation with the man, they shook hands on a deal, and Lyons wrote him a cheque.

"Now, remember the arrangement. I'll bring him down to the marina at ten o'clock on Saturday. Have everything organised OK?" Lyons said.

"Fine. Leave it with me. I'll have it all set up."

* * *

On the following Saturday, at breakfast, Lyons said to her partner, "Mick, will you do something for me today?"

"Sure. What do you want me to do?"

"Just come with me in the car, and don't ask any questions," Lyons said.

"Hmm, OK. But what's all the mystery?" Hays said.

"I thought we said no questions."

"Oh, OK," Hays said. He was clearly uncomfortable, but intrigued all the same.

When they got to the marina at the sailing club, the Beneteau 28 was there with an enormous red ribbon wrapped around it and tied in a bow. A large card with

"To Mick, from Maureen with love" was propped up in the cockpit.

Hays couldn't believe his eyes.

"What the blazes is this?" He turned to Lyons with a big wide grin on his face.

"I hope you don't mind. I traded in your Folkboat. But don't worry, all the stuff has been moved across to this one. It's ready to go once you sign the registration documents."

"God, Maureen. I don't know what to say. You've really taken the wind out of my sails. Thank you. Thank you so much."

He drew her to him and kissed her slowly and softly on the lips.

Character list

Senior Inspector Maureen Lyons – a feisty and determined Garda who always seems to be in trouble.

Superintendent Mick Hays – Lyons' superior officer and life partner.

Chief Superintendent Finbarr Plunkett – a wily old policeman who steers a delicate course to keep everyone happy.

Detective Sergeant Sally Fahy – a young energetic detective with a good sense of humour.

Detective Garda Dermot Heffernan – the newest recruit to the Detective Unit in Galway.

Sergeant Séan Mulholland – a laid back officer who likes to run the Garda station in Clifden at his own pace.

Garda Jim Dolan – an experienced Garda attached to the Clifden station.

Garda Peadar Tobin – Clifden's youngest Garda who is building his reputation.

Garda Pascal Brosnan – the Garda who runs the station in Roundstone.

Garda Mary Fallon – a new recruit who has been sent to Roundstone to double the police presence there.

Garda John O'Connor – the Detective Unit's technologist who loves working with computers and mobile phones to expose wrongdoing.

Joe Mason – the Garda's dog handler.

Brutus – an Alsatian with a great nose for evidence of crime.

Sinéad Loughran – a highly competent forensic officer.

Dr Julian Dodd – a sarcastic but very proficient pathologist.

Eoin O'Malley – an ex-con with his mind set on revenge.

Sheena Finnegan – a civil servant from Clifden who enjoys a night out.

Mr & Mrs Finnegan – Sheena's parents.

Carol Gleeson – Sheena's friend.

Breda Fox – Triona's widowed mother.

Triona Fox – a schoolgirl who doesn't like cycling in the rain.

Jeremiah Breslin – a shifty architect with a small practice on Galway.

Jim Cassidy – a council worker from Clifden.

James McMahon – an architect from Galway with a good reputation.

Edward Mulvaney – the duty solicitor.

If you enjoyed this book, please let others know by leaving a quick review on Amazon. Also, if you spot anything untoward in the paperback, get in touch. We strive for the best quality and appreciate reader feedback.

editor@thebookfolks.com

www.thebookfolks.com

BOOKS BY DAVID PEARSON

In this series:

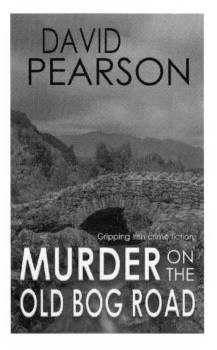

A woman is found in a ditch, murdered. As the list of suspects grows, an Irish town's dirty secrets are exposed. Detective Inspector Mick Hays and DS Maureen Lyons are called in to investigate. But getting the locals to even speak to the police will take some doing. Will they find the killer in their midst?

Available on Kindle and in paperback from Amazon.

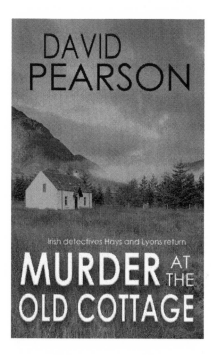

When a nurse finds a reclusive old man dead in his armchair in his tumbledown cottage, the local Garda surmise he was the victim of a burglary gone wrong. However, having suffered a violent death and there being no apparent robbery, Irish detectives Hays and Lyons are not so sure. With no apparent motive it will take all their wits and training to track down the killer.

Available on Kindle and in paperback from Amazon.

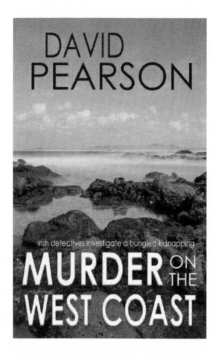

When the Irish police arrive at a road accident, little do
they know it will lead to evidence of a kidnapping and a
murder. Detective Maureen Lyons is in charge of the case
but struggling with self-doubt, and when a suspect slips
through her fingers she must act fast to save her reputation
and crack the case.

Available on Kindle and in paperback from Amazon.

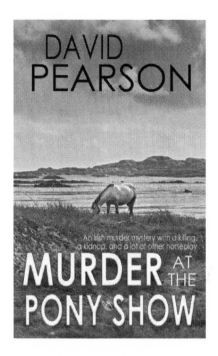

A man is found dead during the annual Connemara Pony Show. Panic spreads through the event when it is discovered he was murdered. Detective Maureen Lyons leads the investigation. But questioning the local bigwigs involved ruffles feathers and the powers that be threaten to stonewall the inquiry.

Available on Kindle and in paperback from Amazon.

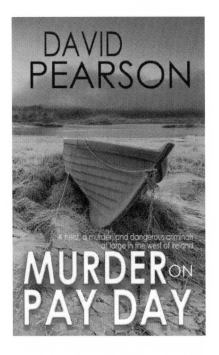

DAVID
PEARSON

A heist, a murder, and dangerous criminals
at large in the west of Ireland

MURDER ON
PAY DAY

Following a tip-off, Irish police lie in wait for a robbery.
But the criminals cleverly evade their grasp. Meanwhile, a
body is found beneath a cliff. DCI Mick Hays' chances of
promotion will be blown unless he sorts out the mess.

Available on Kindle and in paperback from Amazon.

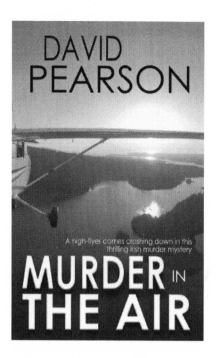

After a wealthy businessman's plane crashes into bogland it is discovered the engine was tampered with. But who out of the three occupants was the intended target? DI Maureen Lyons leads the investigation, which points to shady dealings and an even darker crime.

Available on Kindle and in paperback from Amazon.

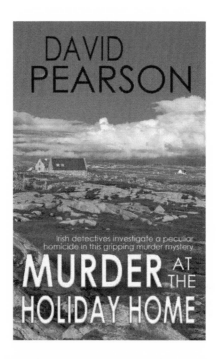

DAVID
PEARSON

Irish detectives investigate a peculiar
homicide in this gripping murder mystery

MURDER AT THE

HOLIDAY HOME

A local businessman is questioned when a young woman is
found dead in his property. His caginess makes him a
prime suspect in what is now a murder inquiry. But with
no clear motive and no evidence, detectives will have a
hard task proving their case. They'll have to follow the
money, even if it leads them into danger.

Available on Kindle and in paperback from Amazon.

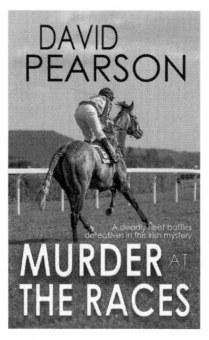

DAVID
PEARSON

A deadly heist baffles
detectives in this Irish mystery

MURDER AT
THE RACES

One of the highlights of Ireland's horseracing calendar is marred when a successful bookmaker is robbed and killed in the restrooms. DI Maureen Lyons investigates but is not banking on a troublemaker emerging from within the police ranks. Her team will have to deal with the shenanigans and catch a killer.

Available on Kindle and in paperback from Amazon.